WILD HONOR

TYSON WILD BOOK EIGHT

TRIPP ELLIS

Copyright © 2019 by Tripp Ellis

All rights reserved. Worldwide.

This book is a work of fiction. The names, characters, places, and incidents, except for incidental references to public figures, products, or services, are fictitious. Any resemblance to persons, living or dead, actual events, locales, or organizations is entirely coincidental, and not intended to refer to any living person or to disparage any company's products or services. All characters engaging in sexual activity are above the age of consent.

No part of this text may be reproduced, transmitted, downloaded, decompiled, uploaded, or stored in or introduced into any information storage and retrieval system, in any form or by any means, whether electronic or mechanical, now known or hereafter devised, without the express written permission of the publisher except for the use of brief quotations in a book review.

WELCOME

Want more books like this?

You'll probably never hear about my new releases unless you join my newsletter.

SIGN UP HERE

1

"What? I can't hear you," I said, shouting over the music, mashing the phone against my ear.

Sheriff Daniels grumbled something.

I couldn't make it out.

I pushed into the salon, weaving through the horde of bikini-clad beauties. Pop music thumped. Pert assets jiggled in rhythm with the beat. Long necks dangled from svelte fingers. Tequila shots flowed freely. Girls licked salt and sucked limes. It was like spring break gone wild.

JD was right about purchasing a luxury party boat...

After spending more than I care to say, we were now host to an endless array of parties. Our clientele ranged from the uber-rich, to social media influencers, to celebrities—anyone who needed to charter a super-yacht for a weekend getaway, party, or fundraising event.

The new boat was nothing short of bad ass.

With a boat like this, it didn't take long to forget about the *Wild Tide*.

I pushed into the en suite, pulled the hatch shut, reducing the music to a dull thump. I could finally hear Sheriff Daniels—not that I really wanted to. "Okay. Sorry. What did you say?"

"I need you, and that wanna-be-reject-rockstar, to get over here as soon as possible."

"What's going on?" I asked.

"You'll see when you get here. 815 Seabreeze Drive. You're going to be plenty pissed off."

"I'm kind of in the middle of something."

"Do I care?"

"We're out on the water. I'll get there as soon as I can."

"Take your time. I don't think the dead guy will mind," Daniels said, his voice thick with sarcasm.

I grimaced. "I'll see you soon."

I hung up the phone, stepped out of the en suite, and weaved through the horde of revelers, looking for JD. I found him on the foredeck applying a shimmering sheen of tanning oil to a toned brunette with olive skin, dark hair, and oversized... *sunglasses*.

"Party is over," I said. "Daniels needs us on shore."

JD's face crinkled. "Can't you see I'm in the middle of a very important operation here. Without the proper application, this young woman could receive a terrible sunburn."

The brunette, Sasha, giggled.

"Homicide," I said.

Sasha's jaw dropped.

JD frowned and grumbled under his breath. He finished rubbing the lotion on the girl's silky skin. "I guess we'll just have to move the party back to the marina."

I shrugged. "I guess."

JD assured the girl that he would continue his duties in the near future. She made a pouty face, exaggeratedly turning out her bottom lip.

Jack Donovan climbed to his feet, and I followed him to the helm.

Jack wore board shorts, a Hawaiian shirt that flowed open in the breeze, and a pair of checkered *Vans*. Dark *Ray Ban* sun glasses covered his eyes. He had long hair that used to be blonde, but was losing the war against the gray. He looked like an '80s rock star, and was often mistaken for one. He had an uncanny resemblance, and Jack never turned down an opportunity to pretend to be famous.

He cranked up the engines, spun the super-yacht around, and headed us back to the marina. People were too busy partying to really notice or care. JD made a quick announcement that we were changing locations. As long as the music kept pumping, and the drinks kept flowing, the party would continue—no matter where we were.

Fortunately this wasn't a paying charter. Jack had decided to throw an impromptu party and handed out flyers to every hot girl he saw on the island. He canvassed all the bars on Oyster Avenue. Of course, Jack considered it a marketing expense—a promotional opportunity to introduce people to the *Vivere* and the new services we offered.

We both knew the amount going out for this new business venture would probably exceed the amount coming in. The super-yacht sounded like a good idea, but it was really just an excuse to buy a *way* too expensive boat. With some creative accounting, we were able to write off the majority of expenses. In theory, the majority of the ship was used for *commercial* services. I let the accountant handle the nitty-gritty. After selling the movie rights to Bree Taylor's story, I needed all the write-offs I could get—after the agency fee, legal fees, and taxes, the seven-figure payday got whittled down quickly.

I told Jack I wanted to name the boat something classy, since we were going for a more upscale clientele. His first suggestion was *Balls Deep,* followed by *Bottoms Up* and *Tequila Bumrise.*

There was a lot of back-and-forth, and I finally convinced him to name the Italian made boat *Vivere*, which means *to live.*

It seemed fitting enough.

At the marina, we tied off the boat and reconnected shore power and water. JD hustled the partiers off the boat, down the dock, and into *Diver Down.* Just a change of venue, Jack assured.

I let Buddy and Fluffy out of the VIP guest suite. The little Jack Russell wagged his tail and bounced around, ready to play. The snobby white cat darted into the hallway. I knelt down and petted Buddy and assured him we'd play later.

I joined Jack at *Diver Down*. Dozens of inebriated partygoers swarmed the bar, and Madison was overwhelmed with drink orders.

Extra business was nice, but she still gave me a dirty look.

I smiled and told her we would be back soon—*official business.*

Her dirty look didn't go away.

We jogged through the parking lot to Jack's new Porsche.

It was a sight to behold.

The lizard green 911 Speedster practically glowed in the dark. It had a sleek, aggressive profile and black satin rims. The flat six made 500 hp, and the car rocketed from 0 to 60 in 3.8 seconds. The black leather interior had lizard green deviated stitching and aluminum accents. It was a beast.

The smell of fresh leather filled my nostrils as I climbed into the car. The bucket seats hugged my form perfectly. The bolsters would keep me firmly in place while cornering at ridiculous speeds. Everything about the car was meticulously crafted to perfection. German engineering at its finest. It was built like a tank, and with the abuse JD would put it through, it needed to be.

Jack twisted the ignition, and the rear engine howled. The car felt fast and powerful just standing still. The speedster had a cloth top—but a car like this deserved to be topless all the time.

Jack let out the clutch, eased out of the parking lot like a jungle cat on the prowl, then floored it as we turned onto the highway. The acceleration pinned me against the seat, and the glorious sound of the exhaust swirled around the cabin. Wind rushed through my hair, and the beast devoured the highway.

This was definitely faster, and nicer, than his last Porsche—and the car was no slouch.

Red and blue lights flickered as we arrived at 815 Seabreeze Drive. A crowd of curious neighbors gathered around the home.

JD parked the car, and we made our way through the horde of onlookers and across the yard. Two officers stood out front, keeping the neighbors at bay as the forensics team did their work inside. There was a mix of worried faces and wide eyes.

Palm trees towered overhead. The home was a small mauve-colored concrete abode that backed up to a canal. You could walk out your back door, hop aboard your boat, and be out on the ocean within minutes.

"What the hell took you so long?" Daniels asked with a scowl as we stepped inside.

Brenda, the medical examiner hovered over the body that lay in the middle of the living room floor. Cameras flashed as a photographer documented the scene.

By this point in time, I had seen just about everything.

Almost nothing fazed me anymore. But this one punched me in the gut.

Sheriff Daniels was right—this did piss me off.

My blood boiled under my skin. I clenched my jaw, and my hands tightened into fists.

Nothing like this should ever happen.

2

Warren Anthony Russell was 92 years old.

There was a World War II era photograph of him on the wall in his Marine Corps dress blues. The image was colorized, and the dapper young man had sparkling blue eyes and a fresh face. He couldn't have been more than 17 or 18 at the time—a far cry from how he looked now.

Warren had been beaten to a pulp, almost beyond recognition. The left side of his face had suffered multiple blows, fracturing the orbital bone and lacerating his thin skin.

Despite his age, he looked rather fit, and had been a handsome man—before the attack.

There was no doubt a beating like this would have caused brain trauma and probably left him with intracranial hemorrhaging. Brenda would give me a full report later, but it didn't take a rocket scientist to figure out the cause of death.

The man was a Medal of Honor recipient. He had stormed the beaches at Normandy. Survived countless encounters with the enemy. Helped to liberate Europe and save America from tyranny. All so some ungrateful thug could beat him to death in his own home in his golden years.

The thought of it made me sick.

It didn't seem fair.

A man like that deserved a peaceful exit, surrounded by family and loved ones—not alone, disrespected by some intruder.

"What have we got?" I asked

"No forced entry," Daniels said. "The back door was ajar and unlocked when we arrived."

"Any witnesses?"

"I've got deputies canvassing the area."

"Motive?"

Daniel shrugged. "Robbery? Mr. Russell could have come home and startled the intruder?"

The place looked ransacked.

I took a quick look around the home. Books had been pulled off of shelves. Drawers had been pulled out. Clothing had been tossed on the floor. Somebody was looking for something.

When I returned to the living room I asked, "Is there anything missing?"

"Hard to say," Daniels replied.

"Do we have any fingerprints? Foot prints?"

"We pulled prints from the door handle, the dresser drawers, various locations around the house," a forensics guy said. "We'll know more later."

"Does he have any immediate family? Wife, kids?" I asked.

"According to our records, his wife is deceased," Daniels said. "She died in '97. He's got a daughter, but she's listed as deceased as well. His granddaughter in Miami got worried when she didn't hear from him. She called the station and asked us to do a wellness check. That's when the deputies found him."

I squatted down beside the body and took a closer look at the man's face. His skin was so thin that it tore easily from the massive blows. There were several bloody impressions around the left cheek and eye. "The assailant was right handed."

"You figure that out all by yourself?" Brenda snarked.

I scowled at her, playfully. "Time of death?"

"Judging by the condition of the body, maybe 9 o'clock last night."

"What are these indentions?" I asked, pointing to Warren's mangled cheek.

"I'm not sure," Brenda said. "The attacker may have been wearing a ring. I'll know more when I take a closer look at the lab."

"See what you can find out," Daniels said. "Somebody had to see something. I want you to get this son-of-a-bitch and nail his ass to the wall."

"With pleasure," I said.

A deputy approached as JD and I stepped outside the home. "I've got a neighbor that lives across the street. She didn't see anything specifically, but she says she was friends with the victim and she thinks she knows who's responsible."

The deputy introduced us to Mrs. Grant. She was an older woman in her late 70s. She was spry and kept herself fit. She wasn't about to let any gray hair show—it was dyed a deep auburn color.

"I'll tell you exactly who you need to be looking for," Mrs. Grant said.

"I'm all ears," I said.

"Warren was such a nice man. Very kind. Too kind. If you ask me, people were taking advantage of him."

"Who?"

"I can't recall her name. Britney, Brandi? Something like that. He was always giving her money, helping her out of tight spots. She's trash, if you want my personal opinion."

"What was the nature of their relationship?" I asked. "Sexual?"

Mrs. Grant gasped and clutched her hand against her chest. "Oh, God no. She's 24, maybe 25? Warren preferred a more sophisticated type of woman."

There was a little sparkle in Mrs. Grant's eyes. I got the impression that, perhaps, she had a fling with Warren—or at least wanted to.

"Did you have a relationship with Warren?" I asked.

Mrs. Grant batted her eyelashes and played coy. "I don't kiss and tell, Deputy Wild."

"Just as a matter of record," I said, urging her to come clean.

"Warren was a real charmer," Mrs. Grant said. "He got along with all the ladies. He was smart, funny, good looking, and he could still *perform*, if you know what I mean. Unassisted. He didn't need any pharmaceuticals."

JD and I exchanged a glance.

"So, I'll note that you had a *casual* relationship," I said.

"We were friends with benefits, you could say. Isn't that what the young kids call it?"

"I'm guessing Warren had a lot of friends?" I asked.

"I would assume so, but I didn't really keep tabs on him."

"This Britany, or Brandi, or whoever… What was her story?" I asked.

A disgusted look twisted on her face. "She always had some sort of crisis going on. She couldn't afford her car note. She couldn't pay her rent. She had outstanding tickets. Personally, I think she just spent the money on drugs and booze. She looked like the type. I think she reminded Warren of his daughter, and he had a soft spot for her. He was always trying to help her get on her feet."

"Is there anyone else you can think of that might have wanted to do Warren harm?"

Her face crinkled like it was the most preposterous thing she'd ever heard. "Warren was a sweetheart. Everybody liked him. He always had a smile, and he was quick to help anyone who asked. If he saw me unloading groceries, he'd always give me a hand. He volunteered as a crossing guard at the middle school. He was always at the nursing home, visiting with residents, trying to keep their spirits up. It's such a downright shame that this would happen to such a nice man!"

Mrs. Grant frowned, and her eyes misted. It had finally hit her that her friend was gone. She casually wiped the tears away. "Warren always joked that he couldn't buy green bananas. At 92, he always said he could go at any minute. He tried to make every moment count."

"When was the last time you saw Britany, or Brandi?" I asked.

Mrs. Grant thought for a moment. "Maybe last week? And it's *Brandi*. It's definitely Brandi. Brandi Lynn something."

"Any idea about her last name?"

"Sorry. Don't have a clue."

"And you haven't seen anyone else coming or going besides Warren?"

She shook her head.

"Nothing strange yesterday?" I asked. "You didn't notice any commotion between 9 and 10 PM?"

"No."

"Where were you at that time?"

"I'm usually in bed by then, watching TV."

I took down her information and told her we might be in touch if we had any more questions.

We talked to a few other neighbors, but no one saw anything.

"Let's see if we can find this *Brandi Lynn*," I said to JD.

I pulled my phone from my pocket and called Denise at the Sheriff's Office. "Hey, I need you to run a search for a Brandi Lynn. Last name unknown. Unpaid tickets. Probably has a criminal history. Mid-20s."

"I'm on it," Denise said.

3

"Brandi Lynn Moore," Denise said. "25, sandy blonde hair, 5'2". Lives at 734 Pelican Way, Apt. #119."

"That could be her," I said.

"She's got priors. Possession of a controlled substance—methamphetamine. Shoplifting. Public intoxication."

"That's definitely our girl. Thanks," I said.

"Anytime."

"Text me her last mug shot."

"You really think she's capable of beating a man to death?" JD asked.

"Never underestimate the ability of people to surprise you," I said. "Besides, if she didn't do it, she may know who did. Look, she regularly goes to Warren for money. Maybe he feels like he's getting used, or maybe he senses that she is using again. He decides to cut her off. That doesn't go over well. Maybe she's got a boyfriend? The boyfriend doesn't want to take *no* for an answer, robs the house, Warren shows up in the middle of it?"

"Or maybe the boyfriend just goes to beat it out of him?" JD said.

"I say we go pay Ms. Moore a visit."

We hopped in JD's Porsche and headed over to her apartment complex.

The Pelican Way apartments were a three story unit with covered parking on the first floor. It was a few blocks off the beach and surrounded by palm trees. The place didn't look run down or shabby. The rent couldn't have been cheap. It was no wonder she needed help from Warren.

A quick call to the main office, and we were buzzed in through the security gate. We strolled to apartment #119 and knocked on the door.

A few moments later, a man yelled through the door in a booming voice, "Who is it?"

Coconut County Sheriff's Deputies. We'd like to speak with Brandi Lynn."

"What's this about?"

I hesitated for a moment. "Warren Russell has been murdered."

There was a long silence.

"You got a warrant?"

"We'd just like to ask her a few questions. Time is of the

essence. She might be able to help us track down his killer." I didn't want to sound too threatening.

I could hear the two of them discussing the situation in hushed tones. A moment later, the door opened. Brandi gazed at me with wide eyes. She fidgeted nervously. I could tell she was strung out.

"Is he really dead?" Brandi stammered.

"Yes, ma'am," I said.

Brandi used to be smoking hot, but the drugs had taken their toll. She answered the door in a bikini top and jean shorts. She could barely fill them out. Her once flawless skin was now full of blemishes. Her cheeks were sunken, and the meth had receded her gums and rotted her teeth. A few were missing. It was such a shame. She was rail thin, and her rib cage was visible.

Her boyfriend had the same sunken look. He hovered in the doorway behind her. He was a big guy. 6'3". Long hair, goatee, sleeved in tattoos. Thin and wiry. The kind of guy who could be dangerous in a bar fight.

I noticed he had a skull ring on his right hand. It could have easily made the impressions on Warren's cheek. I was beginning to think we had found the perpetrators.

"How did he die?" Brandi asked.

I told her.

"Oh, my God. That's terrible!"

She didn't exactly burst into tears, but she *did* look upset.

The two exchanged a wary glance.

"Where were you last night?" I asked, trying to sound casual.

Brandi fidgeted nervously and exchanged another glance with her boyfriend.

"Don't answer that," he said. "You don't have to say shit."

"I didn't catch your name," I said.

"We're not saying anything without an attorney," he barked.

He tried to stare me down, but it didn't work.

"You could really help us solve this crime," I said. "The sooner we find out information, the better."

"This conversation is over." He slammed the door.

Before the door had closed, a wave of concern washed over Brandi's face. They were hiding something. I knew it wouldn't be long before the two of them would unravel.

"They're not acting guilty at all, are they?" JD muttered, sardonically.

"Let's see if we can get a warrant."

I could hear the two of them bickering through the door, but I couldn't make out what was said. I did, however, hear Brandi call her boyfriend *Brad*.

"How cute," I said. "Brandi and Brad. I'm sure he's got a rap sheet." I flashed a wry smile.

We left the apartment building and headed back to the Sheriff's Office. I had Denise search the database for anyone named Brad that had prior convictions in Coconut Key. We hovered around her desk as she scrolled through the list, sifting through mugshots. Her svelte fingers and perfectly manicured nails danced across the keys like a concert pianist.

Phones rang, keyboards clacked, and deputies buzzed about.

The coffee pot was empty—which was considered a felony around these parts.

It didn't take long to find a match. Brad Porter. Assault and battery, domestic violence, grand theft auto, possession of a controlled substance. A real winner.

"That's our guy," I said.

"They seem like a real power couple," Denise said, her voice thick with sarcasm.

"Let's get this information over to Brenda, see if she can match prints from the crime scene with these two," I said.

"Those two dipshits aren't bright enough to cover their tracks," Jack said. "This is going to be open and shut."

Everything was falling into place, and that made me nervous.

4

"We got a partial print on the back doorknob that matches what we have on file for Brad Porter," Brenda said.

A grin tugged at my lips, and I clenched my fist in triumph as I exclaimed, "Yes!"

"Just as you thought, there was intracranial hemorrhaging. He was most likely unconscious at the time of death. I'll let you know if I'm able to pull any prints or DNA from the body."

I thanked Brenda and hung up the phone.

We talked to Sheriff Daniels, then presented the evidence to the district attorney who felt there was enough to move forward. Soon we had a warrant in our hands. JD and I, along with the SWAT team, were ready to kick down Brandi's door at the Pelican Way apartments.

We suited up with bulletproof vests and joined the tactical squad. Clad in black with assault rifles, helmets, and flash bang grenades, the tac-team was ready to breach the apartment.

I knocked on the door and shouted, "County Sheriff! We have a warrant for your arrest."

There was no response.

We waited a few seconds, then two tactical officers slammed a battering ram into the door, knocking it from the hinges. Wood splintered, and the door crashed to the tile in the foyer.

Someone tossed in a flash-bang grenade, and the apartment filled with blinding light and a deafening boom.

Anybody inside would be dazed.

The tactical team flooded in through the haze, the barrels of assault rifles sweeping the area. It was a chaotic few moments as officers cleared the apartment. But when the smoke dissipated, we came up empty-handed.

Brad and Brandi had disappeared. No doubt spooked by our earlier visit.

The two suspects had quickly risen to the top of the county's most wanted list. Daniels put out a BOLO (be on the lookout) for them. An older Ford Taurus was registered in Brandi's name—Brad didn't have a vehicle—and Brandi's car wasn't in the parking garage.

We searched the apartment and found a small stash of marijuana, a few crumbs of what appeared to be methamphetamine, and a couple of pipes, thick with resin.

"They couldn't have gotten too far," Daniels said. "There's

only one way out of the Keys. With any luck, a unit will spot them on Highway 1."

Daniels took notice of my look of disappointment. He patted me on the shoulder, "Don't worry. We'll get them. You boys done good."

It was rare praise from the sheriff.

I called Denise and asked her to look up information on the two suspects—relatives that may be in town, known associates, places of employment, though I doubted either of them had a job. If they weren't heading out of town, maybe they were holding up with a friend? Or maybe they were looking to get off the island by boat?

"If you can get me Brad's or Brandi's cell phone number, I might be able to track the location," I said.

"I'm two steps ahead of you," Denise said. "I already looked into it. Brandi's cell phone has been disconnected for nonpayment, and I haven't been able to find one for Brad. I contacted every cellular provider in the area. He's probably using a prepaid cellular, if he's using anything at all."

"I'm impressed," I said.

"Please," Denise sighed. "Give me a little credit."

"I'll give you all the credit. We wouldn't get anything done without you."

"Damn straight."

I chuckled and thanked her.

"Hey, I'm about to get off my shift. And I think you owe me a beer, or two."

Sheriff Daniels was in earshot, and he knew damn good and well who I was talking to. I'd been keeping my distance from Denise due to the sheriff's policy against interdepartmental romances.

"Yes, that would be great," I said in a formal tone.

"Is Daniels listening?"

"Affirmative."

"Don't be a pussy. It's just a drink. There's no policy against drinks with coworkers. Besides, I have no intention of becoming one of your exes. I'll be at *Aqualung*. Be there or be square." Denise hung up the phone.

I looked at my watch and nudged JD. "You know, it's almost happy hour at *Aqualung*."

His eyes brightened. "Ooh! Great minds think alike."

"You know, I'm going to join you two," Daniels said. "I've been meaning to talk to you both."

I swallowed hard. Were we in trouble? His tone sounded grim.

5

Aqualung was a dive bar—pun intended. The walls were adorned with scuba masks, snorkels, wetsuits, and old dive tanks. There was a wall of customer pictures from the reefs. Some of them were phenomenal—wide angles, pink coral, vibrant fish. The drinks were cheap, and the bartender always had a heavy pour. It wasn't as touristy as some of the other spots on Oyster Avenue.

We sat at a high-top table near the bar. A cute blonde waitress named Rose took our order. She was from a small town in Texas and had a little twang in her voice. She had a delightful smile and reminded me of a young Marilyn Monroe.

Daniels ordered a round of beer, and Denise arrived just about the time Rose brought the frosty long necks to the table.

"Hey, guys," Denise said, clearly surprised to see the sheriff.

Daniels's face twisted with suspicion. "Are you here by coincidence?"

"Can't a girl enjoy a drink in a bar after work?"

Daniels frowned and shot me a look.

I shrugged innocently.

"Can I get you something to drink, doll?" Rose asked.

Denise smiled. "I'll have what they're having."

"Coming right up," Rose said with a bubbly smile.

"Well, now that we're all here…" Daniels had a grim look on his face. "I haven't told anyone this, and I don't really like discussing my personal business—"

"You're not retiring, are you?" I asked.

Daniels glared at me. "And let you two run amok? Hell no."

I chuckled and exhaled a relieved breath. I liked Daniels's no nonsense approach. He could be gruff and stern, but he didn't mince words, and he was a straight shooter.

"I've got an election to win, and I fully intend on serving out another term," the sheriff declared.

"So, what's the news, boss?" JD asked.

Daniels sighed. "My dad is having some issues. He fell the other day. He's 87 years old, and he lives by himself. Got a touch of dementia." He paused. "Seeing Warren Russell beaten like that really got under my skin. I mean, that could have been my dad. Hell, that could be any of us in our golden years."

Daniels huddled over his beer, and there was a somber mood around the table.

"We'll get these scumbags," I said. "It's just a matter of time."

Daniels nodded. "I just don't think I can continue to let Dad live alone. He's okay after the fall—just sore and a few bruises, but it could have gone so many ways of wrong. He's fighting me tooth and nail on this, but I think I've got to move him down here and put him into a facility while he still remembers who I am."

We all cringed.

"He's getting to the point where he needs full-time assistance, and I can't manage it by myself," Daniels continued. "Anyway, I'm not looking for a pity party, I'm just letting you know that I may have to take some time here and there to handle this and get him moved down here. I'll need you all to hold down the fort."

"No problem," I said. "Let us know if there's anything we can do."

"Stay out of trouble and get shit done," Daniels grumbled before taking a sip of his beer.

"Where does he live?" JD asked.

"He's in Texas right now. He doesn't have long-term care insurance. Do you know how much those facilities cost? An arm and a leg. Some of these places are close to $10,000 a month! I don't know how anybody is supposed to afford getting old." Daniels paused. "I'll probably have to sell his house and the ranch to pay for the facility."

"Like I said, let us know if there's anything we can do," I

offered.

"I'm probably going to take next week off to go up there and get things in motion."

"Keep us in the loop," JD said. "Sorry you've got to deal with this."

Daniels shrugged. "It's part of life."

He took a sip of his beer, then wiped the grim look from his face. "Well, enough of the pity party. Let's enjoy the good life while we've got it." He raised his amber bottle, and we clinked long necks.

Daniels finished his beer and called it an early evening.

"I feel so sorry for him," Denise said after he left. "That's just horrible to have to go through. He never talks about anything remotely personal. He must really like you two. I don't think he trusts everyone with that kind of information."

"Fuck that getting old shit. I just want to go out in a blaze of glory," JD said. He raised his beer, and we clinked necks again.

I took a sip of my beer, then looked at my watch. "Oh, shit. I forgot about our party."

"I'm sure they've moved on," JD said.

"You two were having a party, and I wasn't invited?" Denise asked.

"It was just a little impromptu gathering," JD assured. "Besides, I knew you were working, and I didn't want you to feel left out."

He was totally full of shit, and Denise knew it. Her eyes narrowed at him. "Well, I still want to see the new boat. And I expect an afternoon on the water."

"I think we can arrange that," JD said. "But we have a strict dress code on board."

"Don't you mean an *undress* code?"

JD smiled. "Whatever you prefer?"

She rolled her eyes. "Please, you two have already seen it. I don't see what the big deal is?"

She knew damn good and well what the big deal was. Just the thought of Denise in a bikini, or less, made my heart beat faster and clouded my judgment.

"Yes, but it was in a strictly professional setting," JD said.

Denise had used her assets in several prior cases to lure in lecherous perps. During the process, JD and I had inadvertently gotten a glimpse at what was underneath that uniform of hers—and it was a sight to behold.

We were like two kittens who'd been given a bowl of milk. We kept loitering around, hoping for another sip. She had us on a string, and now she was just playing with us. Though, now that I was back on the market, she seemed to be taunting me even more.

"I'm off tomorrow," Denise said. "There's a sandbar party at Barracuda Key."

"I'm there," JD said.

"You boys mind if I bring a friend?"

JD's eyes perked up. "The more the merrier."

6

JD's phone blew up with a few texts. The brunette he was lotioning up earlier requested his services. He showed me her text. "She's upset that I abandoned her." He grinned. "I'm gonna go make it up to her."

Denise rolled her eyes.

Jack slid the phone in his pocket and finished his beer. "You good?"

"I'll catch a cab home."

"I'll take you," Denise said.

"Then I will see you good people tomorrow." Jack gave me a mock salute and strutted out of the bar like a kid on Christmas morning.

"He's something else, isn't he?" Denise muttered. "And what about you? I'm surprised you don't have some hot young thing lined up tonight?"

I looked straight into those gorgeous green eyes of hers. "I do."

She laughed. "Save it, Romeo."

There was a moment of silence, then she brought up the ex. "Have you talked to Reagan?"

"I have. I think she's doing well."

"So, you guys decided not to do the long distance thing?"

"Something like that."

"That's too bad. You seemed rather smitten."

I squirmed a little. "Well, you know, the walls around my heart aren't impenetrable."

"Just difficult to climb?"

"How did I become the topic of conversation here? Surely there are more interesting things to discuss?"

"No need to get defensive," Denise said with a grin.

"What about you? Is there anybody special in your life that you've been hiding away?"

"Denise scoffed. "As if I have time for a relationship. And if I did, I certainly wouldn't tell you two about it."

I pretended to be offended.

"Please, I get enough shit about the guys I date from my father. I don't need it from you guys as well."

"I would never give you shit."

"No, you'd just go beat the guy up if you didn't approve."

"Only if he was an ass."

"Believe me, I've dated a lot of asses."

"Well, maybe one of these days you'll trade up," I said with a cocky grin, then took a sip of my beer.

Denise rolled her eyes. "Newsflash. The whole cocky, charming thing isn't going to work on me."

"If you say so," I said dryly.

She scowled at me playfully.

"Don't worry. I would never break Sheriff Daniels's rule. Besides, you and I would never work, anyway."

Denise arched a curious eyebrow. "And why is that?"

"We just wouldn't. You wouldn't put up with my shit. I wouldn't put up with your shit. We'd be a disaster. I mean, it could be a fun disaster. Tempestuous. Stormy. Dangerous." I smiled.

Denise rolled her eyes again. "Well, I guess we'll never find out."

I acted disinterested, turning slightly away. "I guess so."

"How's Madison?" Denise asked, steering the conversation in a more benign direction.

"She's good."

"Does she know what she's having yet?"

"Nope. She still wants it to be a surprise."

"Do *you* know?" Denise asked, leaning closer.

"No. And I wouldn't tell you if I did." I flashed a smug grin.

She smacked my arm, playfully. "You're just mean."

"No. I'm loyal."

She thought about it for a moment, then sighed, "Okay. I can't argue with that."

"Can I get you another round?" Rose asked, strolling by at just the right moment.

"No thanks," Denise said. "I'm dangerously close to poor life decisions as it is."

Rose laughed. "I'll be back with the tab."

When Rose returned, Denise snatched the check before I could get to it. "I can pay for my own drinks."

"I thought I owed you a beer, or two?"

"I think I like having you in my debt."

I raised my hands in surrender. "Far be it from me to pass up free alcohol."

Denise stuffed a wad of cash inside the leather folio and left a healthy tip.

We left *Aqualung* and stepped onto the sidewalk. It was a Saturday night, and the avenue bustled with activity. Revelers strolled up and down the sidewalks, hopping from bar to bar. The glow from neon signs painted the avenue in an array of colors. Music from live bands echoed through the thick night air.

We strolled down the block to her yellow SUV, and I

climbed in the passenger seat. We headed back to the marina, and she pulled her vehicle around to the dock.

"Thanks again for the drinks," I said.

"My pleasure."

"Next round is on me. I insist."

I hesitated a moment before hopping out of the car. I wanted to invite her aboard, but thought that might be a bad idea. Fuck it. Why not? "You want to see the boat?"

Her eyes narrowed at me, skeptical. "I'll see it tomorrow."

"Good. Because I didn't really want to show it to you tonight, anyway."

She scowled at me. After a moment of thought, she said, "Just a *tour* of the boat. That's all. *Not* a tour of your stateroom."

I shrugged innocently. "You have a dirty mind."

She sneered at me, then looked out over the water. Her eyes widened, and she pointed to the super-yacht. "That's not it, is it?"

7

"Holy shit, that's big!" Denise exclaimed as we strolled down the dock to the *Vivere*.

I couldn't resist the urge to mutter, "That's what she said."

Denise smacked my arm, playfully.

"It's only 8 feet longer than the *Wild Tide*."

JD's impromptu party had long since dissipated, and none of the original horde of revelers remained in *Diver Down*.

The waves lapped against the hull, and the boats in the marina gently swayed. We crossed the retractable gangway, traversing over the swim platform which held an 8 foot tender. We stepped aboard the aft deck of the *Vivere* and Denise's eyes lit up with awe.

"Wow! This is nicer than your other boat."

"Thank you."

There was a U-shaped lounge in the aft deck with an

alfresco dining area. The Hi-Lo table was topped in carbon fiber. There was aft storage under the settee and several refrigerated compartments about the cockpit. A summer galley with a grill made cookouts on the water a breeze. Steps on either side led down to the hydraulic swim platform. A port-side staircase led up to the flybridge which was complete with a second helm, a lounge area, minibar, and a jacuzzi.

Through the sliding glass door, we entered the salon.

Buddy greeted us with excitement, tail wagging, bouncing like a maniac. Denise knelt down and loved on the energetic pooch.

There was a sofa to port and starboard, and a Hi-Lo flatscreen TV to port. Forward, there was a minibar with glassware stowage, a refrigerator, and an ice maker. To port was the dining area. Forward of that was a day head to port, across from the galley. There was a two-seat helm control with touchscreen displays, joystick control of the bow and stern thrusters, and every conceivable nautical gadget. To port of the helm was another small lounge area with an L-shaped settee and a Hi-Lo table.

The boat had elegant curves and sleek lines. Large windows bathed the interior with light on sunny afternoons. A centerline staircase led to the lower deck, which contained a full beam master suite with a queen birth and en suite. There were two VIP guest suites with queen births and private en suites, and another guest suite with four stacked twins and an en suite. Two crew compartments were located aft of the engine room.

The overall length was 80'6" with a 22'4" max beam. The

draft was 6'2" at full load. Two 1800 MHP V12 engines gave the *Vivere* a max speed of 28 knots.

There was another lounge on the foredeck with a U-shaped setee, carbon fiber cocktail table, and large sunpads. A retractible electric awning provided shade when needed.

The craftsmanship was impeccable, and only the finest materials were used.

The boat was a wreck after the party—empty beer cans and drink glasses everywhere.

"You'll have to excuse the mess," I said.

Buddy finally calmed down. I gave Denise a tour, and her luscious green eyes took in the opulent appointments.

"I have to admit, this is really nice. You two have outdone yourselves."

"Not bad for a starter yacht," I said with a grin.

She chuckled. "I'd say."

There was a long pause as our eyes lingered on each other.

"Well, I guess I will see you tomorrow?"

"We'll have fun! JD can regale you with tales of pirate treasure."

"Is he still looking for that?"

"Oh, he's serious about it. We lost our remote sonar scanner on the *Wild Tide,* but he's got another one on order. He's determined to find the lost fortune of the great pirate Jacques De La Fontaine."

"And what are you two going to do when you find it?"

I shrugged. "Raise hell, drink margaritas, chase women."

"Isn't that exactly what you do now?"

I smiled. "Pretty much. But the hunt is half the fun."

She grinned. "Yes, it is."

Denise spun around and sauntered toward the aft deck. She had a nice saunter.

"Sure you don't want to stay for one drink?" I asked.

She looked back over her shoulder as she reached the glass sliding door. "Like I said, I'm one drink away from poor life decisions."

"Then maybe you should have two?" I suggested.

"Good night, Tyson."

She slid open the door and stepped into the cockpit. Denise traversed the gangway, and I stepped to the aft deck, watching her as she strolled to her vehicle. There was no longer a serial killer running around Coconut Key, but you could never be too careful.

Buddy's paws clacked against the deck as he joined me. I knelt down and petted him, and he basked in the attention. I leashed him up and took him for a walk. Afterward, I cleaned up the boat, then settled into bed for the evening.

Buddy curled beside me.

I was still getting used to the new digs. The boat didn't quite feel like home yet, but that was only a matter of time. I watched a little TV, catching a replay of the *MotoXP* race before sacking out.

The morning sun burst through the array of square portholes, filling the room. I yawned, stretched, and staggered out of bed. I pulled on board shorts and made my way to the galley and fixed breakfast.

JD arrived as I downed the last of the scrambled eggs. His face crinkled. "You didn't save any for me?"

"You should have told me you wanted breakfast."

Jack frowned.

He moved into the galley and poured himself coffee, then sauntered back to the dining table and took a seat across from me. "Do we have enough beer?"

"I think we have plenty enough to get us through the day."

"One can never be too prepared."

"There's whiskey and rum once the beer runs out."

"Do we have any idea about this friend of Denise's? Do you think she's hot?"

I shrugged. "They tend to run in packs, so I'm guessing so."

A devious smile curled on Jack's lips.

"How did things go with the brunette last night?" I asked.

"Dude... Have I got a story for you."

"I can only imagine."

"So, I get over to her place. One thing leads to another, and we're going at it hot and heavy on the couch. Her little

Chihuahua is sitting there watching the whole thing, looking up at me with those eyes, thinking *you mother fucker.* I usually have a rule about women with small yappy dogs, but that's another story entirely. Then the roommate walks in the door.

"We're buck naked.

"Sasha doesn't even stop. She's going for broke.

"The roommate, Tasha, is 5'3", blonde, got one of those fitness bodies. She's wearing a lacy black top, a black miniskirt that barely covers her hootenanny, and 6" *fuck me* pumps.

"She stops and watches for a moment. Then she says, *looks like fun."*

"And...?" I asked.

JD was about to continue the story when Denise showed up with her friend, Jordyn.

Wow!

Jordyn was nothing short of stunning. A blonde haired, blue-eyed goddess with all-natural assets that defied gravity.

Jack and I both lost our trains of thought, and our jaws hit the floor. We tried to shovel our tongues back into our mouths as the girls strutted across the gangway and into the cockpit.

The two girls wore skimpy sundresses and carried tote bags with beach towels, sunscreen, and whatever else they might need.

This was certainly going to be an interesting day.

8

Denise introduced Jordyn, and JD got the girls a beer.

"This is an impressive boat," Jordyn said.

"Thank you," JD replied.

"I could get used to this."

"I'm sure we could get used to you being here."

Jordyn smiled.

We disconnected shore power and water, then cast off the lines. JD took the helm and idled out of the marina. It was a beautiful start to the day. Gulls hung on the breeze overhead. The sun glimmered across the water, and there wasn't a cloud in the sky.

JD throttled up the boat, and we plowed through the water like a freight train, leaving a frothy trail of white water.

Jordyn peeled off her sundress, and the ring spun cotton hit the deck.

I tried not to stare.

The fabric of her skimpy bikini screamed for mercy. Her pert breasts begged for liberation. They were determined to spring free of the overstuffed teeny bikini. I was sure a wardrobe malfunction would happen at some point during the day.

Not to be outdone, Denise followed suit.

My God, the two of them standing there, wearing barely nothing, was almost too much to handle. I wasn't complaining, mind you. I used my best covert skills to soak in every sumptuous curve without being too obvious about it—I pretended to act thoroughly disinterested.

The girls knew better.

"Denise tells me you work together at the Sheriff's Office."

I nodded.

"You're the guy who caught the *Sandcastle Killer,* right?"

I nodded again.

Her eyes brightened. "That sounds so exciting!"

I shrugged. "I guess."

"I can see why Denise has been keeping you all to herself."

Denise's cheeks flushed, and she glared at Jordyn.

Jordyn knew she was embarrassing Denise and decided to keep going. "She can't stop talking about you, you know?"

I pretended to be surprised. "Really? I had no idea."

I gave a cocky glance to Denise.

"Jordyn has an overactive imagination," Denise said.

"Oh, come on! You're always going on about him. *Tyson this... Tyson that...*"

I tried not to grin too much.

Denise squinted at me and shook her head. "Don't pay attention to her. She likes to cause trouble."

"Who me?" Jordyn asked, innocently.

"Yes, you!" Denise replied. "You promised to behave."

Jordyn smiled. "Please, a little mischief is good for the soul." A naughty glimmer flickered in her eyes. "If I get out of line, Tyson can always handcuff me and throw me in a cell for bad girls." She said in a pouty voice. Jordyn jiggled her bum. "I don't mind a little punishment."

Denise shook her head.

"I'll go look for my handcuffs."

"Don't encourage her," Denise said.

It didn't take long to reach Barracuda Key Island. The sandbar party was in full effect. Hundreds of small boats were anchored in the shallow water. A sea of revelers waded in the teal sea.

The draft of the *Vivere* was too deep for the shallow water above the sandbar. We anchored the boat offshore and took the tender into the shallows. We loaded up with beer, snacks, and bottled water.

People mixed and mingled in the waist deep water, drinking beer and taking Jell-O shots. There were all types, ranging from tanned hard summer bodies to soft couch potatoes.

Wild Honor

There were jiggling fleshy mounds, rippled abs, beer bellies, oversized bodybuilders, bald sunburned heads, and pasty white tourist skin that hadn't seen the sun in a year. It was mostly locals, but a few vacationers had been clued into the scene.

A live band cranked out classic rock from a pontoon boat.

The sandbar was maybe 50 yards from the pristine beach—white sand and palm trees.

The water was warm, and the air smelled like barbecue. People floated around on giant ducks, inflatable pink flamingos, inner tubes, rafts, and floating lounge chairs. A massive beach ball bounced around the crowd.

I climbed out of the tender into the waist deep water, and the girls followed suit. We anchored the inflatable boat, grabbed a few beers from the ice chest, and mingled through the crowd.

Partiers bonged beer, funneling 12 ounces down their throats in less than a second. They swigged from bottles of whiskey or tequila, bounced in rhythm to the music, and let their cares float away.

This kind of thing happened every weekend, though the crowds were always bigger on holidays.

The sandy bottom conformed to the soles of my feet as I trudged through the shallow water.

A tanned brunette strolled by, wearing a skimpy bikini and carrying a giant squirt gun. "Do you want a shot?"

"Hit me," Jordyn said.

She opened her mouth, and the brunette aimed the squirt

gun which looked like a futuristic space weapon. Her manicured fingers squeezed the trigger twice, squirting an unknown liquor into Jordyn's mouth.

Jordyn guzzled it down and gasped afterward. She shouted an excited, "Whooo!"

It wasn't even noon yet, and Jordyn was ready to get rowdy. She grabbed my hand and pulled me through the water. "Let's go see the band!"

I looked over my shoulder at Denise, who had a perturbed look on her face.

I shrugged innocently and flashed an apologetic smile.

We weaved through the crowd, moving closer to the band barge. Jordyn bounced around, dancing to the beat.

"So, what's the real story between you and Denise?" Jordyn asked.

"No story."

"She swears you two haven't hooked up, but I'm not sure I buy it."

"We're coworkers. That would be against office policy."

She scoffed. Then she asked with a mischievous grin, "Don't you ever break the rules, Mr. Wild?"

I didn't answer.

"Well, it's a good thing we don't work together." She grabbed my arm and pulled herself close "I don't know how long I could hold out."

She looked up at me with her gorgeous blue eyes and batted her lashes. This girl oozed sensuality.

"Don't you think that might upset Denise?"

"So, there *is* something going on?"

"No."

"I mean, she told me you were fair game. She wasn't going to break *office policy*," Jordyn said with air quotes.

"*Fair game*, huh?"

Jordyn danced away with a grin, putting in extra jiggle in her assets, taunting me.

Two girls floated by on a giant pink flamingo and handed her an orange Jell-O shot. Jordyn slurped it out of the plastic container. It was probably safe, but I never ingested anything from strangers. You never really knew what was in it.

Jordyn was definitely a free spirit. She bounced back toward me with a devious glimmer in her eyes. She twirled around, parked her glorious cheeks against my hips, and twerked. She bent over and ground her assets against me.

Too much more of that, and I might have to take her up on her offer.

The last thing I needed was to create an awkward situation with Denise. We had a good working relationship, and I didn't want to screw that up. Banging her friend at a sandbar party might not be a good idea.

Jordyn was quite enticing, and I don't think too many men ever told her *no*.

She stood up, raised her hands in the air and twirled around, then backed away a few steps, teasing me. She was working it pretty hard. And for a moment, I wondered if this was a setup? Did Denise tell her friend to hit on me to see if I would take the bait?

I peeled my eyes away from her gorgeous body, pretending to be disinterested. I should have gotten an Academy Award™ for my performance. I glanced around at the sea of revelers enjoying life at its finest.

I did a double take at what I saw.

9

The tall, thin man with long hair stood out in a crowd. Brad Porter already had a good sunburn working.

I gritted my teeth and clenched my fists.

It was a rare occasion that I wasn't armed. The only thing I had was a mostly empty beer and my swim trunks.

I plowed through the water, heading toward the scumbag. He was with Brandi. The two of them were wasted.

Brad just happened to catch sight of me. His eyes widened, and he took off, sloshing through the crowd.

You can only run so fast in 3 feet of water.

I chased after him, my legs driving me forward.

Brad pulled a man from a *SeaCycle* and climbed aboard. He cranked the engine up, twisted the throttle, and plowed forward. The exhaust rattled, and water sprayed from the back-end. He tried to weave through the crowd, but mowed over a few partygoers along the way.

The man's girlfriend sat on her cycle in shock at what had just happened. A stream of expletives flew from the man's mouth as Brad sped away.

"County Sheriff," I shouted. "I need to borrow your watercraft."

The girl climbed off, and I hopped on. I cranked the engine up and twisted the throttle.

By this point in time, the horde of revelers had parted. People attended to those who'd been run over by Brad. Mostly bruises, abrasions, and lacerations.

The wind whistled my ears as I raced across the surface on the *SeaCycle*. Mists of saltwater sprayed into the air.

The 300 hp, supercharged engine propelled me forward at a blistering pace. It had a 0 to 60 time of 3.8 seconds, every bit as fast as Jack's Porsche. It had a closed-loop cooling system to keep corrosion and debris at bay. It had a V-shaped hall that allowed it to carve around corners, making it quick and nimble. With an active braking system, the craft could stop considerably faster than most vessels.

Engineered to perfection, these *SeaCycles* weren't cheap.

The swells were small, but occasionally acted like a ramp and launched the craft into the air. The engine howled during the hang time before crashing back against the water. I followed the frothy white trail ahead of me, chasing after Brad.

I don't think he had a destination in mind. Anywhere but here.

With the throttle pegged, the watercraft skimmed across the surface.

The sandbar became a distant memory.

Salt water sprayed me in the face. I ducked low behind the windscreen and tried to extract every ounce of power out of the watercraft. The two vehicles were evenly matched, and I wasn't narrowing the gap.

Then the unthinkable happened.

The engine coughed and sputtered, then conked out.

The *SeaCycle* sloshed against the swells, drifting with the current.

An explosion of unsavory words spewed from my lips, and I

pounded my fist against the handlebars.

Brad's trail of white water dissipated amidst the swells, and soon, the watercraft disappeared on the horizon. The whine of its engine faded in the distance.

I looked back to the sandbar. I had traveled farther than I realized. The swarm of revelers looked like tiny specks in the water. I could barely hear the echo of the music, and the snap of the snare drum, across the sea.

My cell phone was back on the *Vivere*.

The swim back to shore was doable, but I didn't want to leave the watercraft unattended. I floated amidst the swells for a few moments to see what developed.

I guess Jordyn had told JD what happened. Before long, they were heading my way in the tender. I watched the little inflatable bounce across the water, the electric outboard humming.

JD pulled alongside the *SeaCycle*.

"Call Sheriff Daniels," I said. "Let him know we saw Porter. And Brandi is still roaming around the crowd somewhere."

We hooked a line to the *SeaCycle* and towed it back to the sandbar. The owner was relieved to get it back, but still disturbed about the loss of the other watercraft. I told them they could file a police report when Sheriff Daniels arrived.

Someone had taken the injured people back toward Coconut Key for treatment. The event had caused a lull in the party, but things had returned to normal by the time we made it back. For most people, there was still plenty of daylight and drinking to do.

JD and I searched the crowd for Brandi, but came up empty-handed.

We waited for the sheriff to arrive. He took statements from witnesses, and the couple that had experienced the theft filled out a report.

Daniels had already alerted the Coast Guard to the situation, and they sent a patrol boat to scour the area for Brad.

After another look around the sandbar for Brandi, Daniels decided to join the Coast Guard in the search for Porter.

At this point, there wasn't much more we could do.

I wasn't much in the mood to party after that. What Porter had done to Warren Russell just burned me up inside. All the memories of my parents' murder came flooding back. I had complete and utter disdain for anyone who would abuse the elderly. My parents weren't near the age of Warren when they were murdered, but the old war hero's death hit close to home.

"Should we go back to the *Vivere* and join the search?" I suggested.

"Look, this whole thing chaps my ass as much as it does yours, but they'll find him," JD assured. "He won't get very far. Besides, you're going to burn out if you keep going like this. You need to let off some steam. It's not always your fight."

I sighed and frowned for a moment. JD was right. It was hard for me to separate from the job. These weren't just random cases. They all somehow became personal. Each crime was a way to redeem myself for the sins of my past. But I didn't really know how the game worked, or who was keeping score? I just knew I'd been given a second chance at life, and I somehow needed to make it count.

JD grabbed an ice cold beer from the chest. Compressed air hissed as he twisted the top and handed the sweaty bottle to me.

Jordyn started massaging my neck, squeezing my traps with her svelte fingers. It felt heavenly. "Relax a little. You deserve it."

Denise's jealous eyes narrowed.

"I'll give you a real massage when we get back to the boat," Jordyn said.

She squeezed my traps again, then grabbed my ass before

sauntering to the tender and grabbing another beer from the ice chest.

"Grab me one, would you?" Denise asked.

Jordyn snatched another beer, then moved through the water to join Denise.

Two tanned guys who looked like they spent a lot of time in the gym walked by, and Denise pretended to stumble into them. "Whoops, I'm sorry."

"No trouble at all," the blond guy said.

"I'm Denise. And this is Jordyn."

I knew exactly what she was doing.

"I'm Nick, and this is Cooper."

Cooper had dark hair, blue eyes, chiseled features, and a day's worth of stubble. "We've got Jell-O shots on the boat. You girls should join us."

"We'd love to," Denise said.

She grabbed Jordyn's hand and pulled her along, strolling away with the guys that had perfect teeth and rippled abs. With her other arm, Denise clung onto Cooper's bicep. She casually glanced over her shoulder at me and gave me a *two can play at that game* look.

I went from getting a sensual back rub to being empty-handed in the blink of an eye.

"Dude, you're fucking up," JD said.

"How am I fucking up? I didn't do anything."

He pointed to Jordyn. "That one is a night of fun." Then he pointed to Denise. "That one is a lifetime of fun. Figure it out."

I sneered at him. "Like you're one to give relationship advice."

"Just saying... I know a keeper when I see one."

"Said the man with six ex-wives."

10

The girls had been gone for a long time, and I decided to go looking for them. I waded through the water while JD held down the fort at the tender.

The blistering sun was high overhead, and by this time of day, several unlucky partygoers were roasted red.

The band had taken a break, and a DJ was spinning EDM tunes. It was like a giant rave. People undulated in rhythm to the beat. I'm sure there were more than a few illicit substances going around. The sweet smell of marijuana wafted through the air.

I'd be lying if I said I wasn't worried about the girls.

These parties were pretty tame for the most part, and everyone usually behaved themselves. But occasionally, things got out of hand. Sometimes passed out girls got taken advantage of. Occasionally, you'd hear about someone who got roofied. It didn't happen often, but it was something that stuck in the back of my mind.

Denise was a sharp girl. She could take care of herself. But sometimes a situation can turn bad quickly.

I finally found them aboard a small 25 foot double-hull. Nick's tongue was down Jordyn's throat, and I can't say I was too surprised. She was looking to have a little fun, and I don't think she was too particular about who it was with.

Denise seemed relieved to see me. Her eyes connected with mine, and I could tell she was uncomfortable.

"We're about ready to get out of here," I said. "Are you staying, or are you going?"

"We're going!" Denise stated.

"They're staying," Cooper said. He looked to Denise and begged. "Come on. The party is just getting started. You don't want to leave now?"

Jordyn was still sucking face with Nick.

Denise tugged her arm. "Come on. We're going."

"I don't want to go," Jordyn said.

"I'll make sure she gets back to the island," Nick said.

Denise forced a smile. "I am not leaving her alone with you guys. Sorry."

"Aw, come on. We're trustworthy. I'm not going to do anything she doesn't want to do."

"There's nothing I don't want to do," Jordyn slurred.

Denise pulled her hand. "Come on. I think you've had a little too much to drink."

"Pfft! Nonsense. I'm perfectly sober."

Jordyn was anything but sober.

"You go," Jordyn urged. "I'll be fine."

"Sorry. I never leave anyone behind."

Cooper grabbed Denise's arm. "You don't really want to go. Do you?"

"Yes. I do." She jerked free.

"Fine. Get the fuck off my boat, bitch!"

Denise arched an eyebrow at him. It was the wrong thing to say to a feisty red-head. "Excuse me? What did you just call me?"

"You heard me. Get off my boat, you little prick tease."

Rage boiled on Denise's face.

I was about two seconds away from losing my temper. "Denise, ignore this douchebag. Come on."

"Yo, what the fuck did you just say?" Cooper growled, puffing up.

"I called you a douchebag. I'm sure you're very familiar with the term."

Cooper clenched his jaw and stormed to the gunwale. He jumped off the boat and into the water, bowing up to me. In a flash, two of his buddies joined him. They quickly surrounded me in the waist deep water.

"I think you just made a big mistake, dick-head," Cooper snarled.

I sighed. "Get back on your boat. Save yourself the trouble."

"Who the fuck do you think you are?" Cooper barked.

"Deputy Sheriff. I don't think you boys want to start shit."

"I don't see a fucking badge," Cooper said, sneering at me.

"Last warning. Get back on the boat. Enjoy the rest of your afternoon."

"Or what? What are you going to do?" Cooper mouthed off.

"Put you in the hospital," I said, blazing into his eyes.

I stared him down, watching his two comrades out of the corner of my eye. I didn't think the guy was smart enough to back down, but to my surprise, he took a step back. "Fuck it. Not worth my time."

Jordyn's cheeks bulged, and her eyes rounded. She leaned over the gunwale and hurled into the water.

A collective groan filled the air.

"Dude, that could have been in my mouth," Nick muttered, backing away from the floating mass of vomit.

"Yeah, get these bitches off my boat," Cooper said, trying to act tough again.

I helped Jordyn and Denise off the boat. I gave the douche-crew a dirty look, then left with the girls. Denise helped Jordyn through the water. She could barely walk. Jordyn heaved again, and I quickly got out of the way of the floating sludge.

We made it back to the tender, and I lifted her aboard. She sprawled out, leaning against the inflatable sides, moaning.

We climbed aboard, and JD cranked up the electric Barracuda motor and we headed back to the *Vivere*.

The hydraulic swim platform was submerged, and we pulled the tender to the stern and tied off. I climbed out and raised the swim platform, then scooped Jordyn in my arms and carried her up the steps to the aft deck and into the salon. I set her down on the sofa, then found a trashcan and set it beside her in case she needed to make an emergency deposit.

Denise sat beside her, trying to comfort her.

JD moved to the helm, cranked up the engines, weighed anchor, and headed us back toward Coconut Key.

After a day in the sun, I was sufficiently baked. Even with plenty of sunscreen, I felt like I'd been cooked.

Jordyn groaned as the boat undulated across the water. The motion wasn't doing anything for her spinning head. She heaved a few more times into the trashcan and passed out somewhere along the way.

"I'm sorry," Denise said to me. "She can get out of hand sometimes."

"I see that."

"She can be a lot of fun, that's why I brought her. I thought you two might get along."

"I didn't think you liked the idea of us getting along?"

"I thought it would be a good idea, then it turned into a bad idea. Then I acted like a jealous high school girl. Which created a mess. Sorry."

I shrugged it off. "No big deal. All's well that ends well."

"Those guys were real dicks."

"You think?"

Denise paused for a long moment. "I like you, Tyson. I just can't get involved with you."

I didn't say anything.

"I don't want to be another ex-girlfriend." Her cheeks flushed. "And I'm certainly not going to be your rebound from Reagan."

"What rebound? That's ancient history."

Denise rolled her eyes. "Maybe I shouldn't be having this conversation with you right now. I've had a little too much to drink, and I think I'm about to be painfully honest."

There was another long, awkward pause.

"Can we just pretend today never happened?"

"I don't remember a thing." I smiled.

"Good." Then she frowned. "I think maybe we shouldn't hang out in social settings anymore. It's probably not good for either one of us. We should just stick to keeping our relationship professional."

My throat tightened. "Professional. Right."

"Besides. We both know you are not the girlfriend type."

I couldn't really argue with her, but I could certainly make an exception for someone like Denise. She was smart, funny, sexy, and she had this wholesome quality about her. She would always shoot it to you straight, and she would never go behind your back. If she was mad, she would tell you, *and tell you why*—and find a way to work through it. I couldn't help but feel like we were closing the door on something that had potential.

11

We made it back to the marina, and I helped Denise escort Jordyn from the couch, down the dock, to the parking lot. She slurred something as she climbed into the Uber, but it was indecipherable.

Denise gave me a hug and kissed me on the cheek before she slipped into the car. She pulled the door shut, and the car whisked them away. I strolled back down the dock as the sun was hanging low over the horizon. The sky was a beautiful array of colors—pink, blue, and purple. I crossed the gangway to the aft deck and took a seat in the lounge with JD in the dining area.

"Daniels called. Came up empty-handed. Porter got away."

I groaned.

"I thought for sure they'd catch that little bastard." Jack could see the distress in my face. "Don't worry. A nitwit like that won't be able to evade capture for long."

We sat in the cockpit, sipping beer, watching the sunset. Seagulls hung in the air.

"What are you up to this evening?" Jack asked.

I shrugged. "I don't know. I think I'm just going to chill. What about you?"

"I think I'm going to try to orchestrate a repeat of last night." He pulled out his phone and clacked around the keyboard, sending a text message. He set the phone atop the carbon fiber table and waited for a reply.

"That good, huh?"

"You have no idea." He took a sip of beer, then changed subjects. "So, Tuesday's the big day?"

"Yup."

"Scarlett says she's all packed and ready." He exhaled a worried breath. "This is crazy. Am I insane to let her do this?"

"I don't think you really have a choice, do you?"

JD's face crinkled. "Well, I've been taking a hands-off approach. I am trying not to influence her one way or another."

"I think that's a good thing. She needs to make her own decisions. Find her own way in life."

"You and I both know she has a habit of finding the wrong way."

"It's part of life. Bad choices become life lessons."

Jack rolled his eyes.

"Why don't you just take her out there?"

"Nope. That's all you. You've got a better handle on that place than I do, and I'm not into the long goodbye. I told her I'd pay for the apartment and send her a little money until she got on her feet, but I'm cutting off the gravy train after three months. That ought to be enough time to find a job and get an affordable apartment."

"Affordable? In Los Angeles?"

"That temporary apartment your agent set her up with costs an arm and a leg. *Oakmont*, or whatever the hell it's called?"

"It's a nice place. It's furnished. A lot of the celebrities stay there from time to time."

"For the price I'm paying, it better be the Taj Mahal."

JD's phone dinged with a text, and the screen lit up. He snatched it from the tabletop and grinned as he read the message. "Well, dreams really do come true."

He finished his beer, stood up, and gave me a salute as he strolled across the gangway.

I stayed in the cockpit for a moment, watching the sunset. Then I went into the salon, found Buddy and leashed him up. I took the little Jack Russell for some much needed exercise. Afterwards, I stopped in *Diver Down* and took a seat at the bar. Harlan was in his usual seat. The old Marine had been there all day. It was a Sunday night, and the crowd was pretty thin—mostly regulars.

Madison was behind the bar wearing a tank top and jean shorts—barefoot as usual. She was 10 weeks pregnant and just barely had a bump.

The news anchor, Emma Steele, was on the flatscreen television behind the bar, talking about the death of Warren Russell. "Police are still searching for a suspect that may be connected to the case."

"You any closer to catching that bastard?" Harlan asked.

"We'll get him. Don't worry."

"That kind of thing just chaps my ass," Harlan said.

Harlan was no spring chicken anymore, and I could tell it hit close to home.

"I mean, what the hell is the world coming to? Let that son-of-a-bitch try to mess with me. I'll fill him full of lead!"

I had no doubt that Harlan was packing.

"Hey Maddy, do you think you could look after Buddy and Fluffy for me when I go to Los Angeles?"

"Sure thing. Just bring them by before you leave."

"Thank you."

"What are you going out to *Hollyweird* for?" Harlan asked.

"Scarlett got an agent. She's going to give the acting thing a go."

"Tell her I said *break a leg*. That's what they say, right?"

I smiled. "I'll tell her."

I left the bar and went back to the *Vivere*. My agent, Joel, called. "Is everything still on for Tuesday?"

"Yep."

"Excellent. How long are you staying in town for?"

"A few days, maybe."

"Good. I've got meetings set up. The studio has a draft of the script for the Bree Taylor story based on your notes. I'll send a PDF shortly. They want to go over it with you. Also, they want to talk TV series. What time do you get in?"

"About 12:30-ish PM your time."

"Give me a call after you get settled, then maybe you two can swing by the office."

"Will do," I said.

I chilled out for the rest of the evening. Monday was uneventful—still no sign of Porter. Tuesday rolled around, and I caught a cab over to Jack's to pick up Scarlett. I packed a small carry-on case, but Scarlett had two full size bags that were loaded to the gills. They weighed more than a baby rhinoceros. "What the hell do you have in these things?"

She huffed. "Tyson, I'm going for a few months. Maybe indefinitely. This is light."

I helped the cab driver load them into the trunk. He groaned as he shoved them in.

JD stood on the driveway with his eyes misting. He tried to remain stoic. Scarlett gave him a hug, and he held onto her for a moment. "You be good out there. Make us proud."

"I will. I love you, Dad."

It was a rare admission from Scarlett, and it almost sent Jack over the edge. He broke free of the embrace, held his breath, and tried not to turn into a blithering idiot.

We climbed into the backseat of the car, and Jack waved as he watched us drive away.

It was in my contract with the studio that they would always provide a charter and first class accommodations when I had meetings. Flying commercial from Coconut Key could be a nightmare. There were no direct flights, and it was easy to get delayed. With one stop, the quickest flight was 9 hours and change. Flying private, the flight time was estimated at 4 hours 27 minutes.

We made our way to the FBO and boarded the *SkyStream X740* jet. Scarlett had never flown on a private plane before, and she was giddy with excitement. The jet was elegantly appointed. Plush leather seats, mahogany trim, flatscreen displays, stocked bar, and an attentive staff.

The captain greeted us with a smile. "Welcome aboard. I'm Captain Williams. We should have a smooth flight. I don't expect much turbulence. I'll have you to Los Angeles in no time. Sit back and enjoy the flight. If you need anything, don't hesitate to ask."

He disappeared into the cockpit, and we slid into the luxurious seats. The smell of fresh leather filled the cabin.

"Jeez, Tyson. You must be somebody," Scarlett exclaimed.

"Perks of doing business with the studio."

Scarlett had stars in her eyes. They glimmered as she soaked in the experience. "One day, they'll be giving me perks."

"I have no doubt."

12

We landed at the private terminal at the Burbank airport. The same limo driver that had chauffeured me around last time waited with a sign. I recognized him instantly. I smiled and shook his hand. "Zaven, right?"

"Yes, sir. Welcome back."

I introduced him to Scarlett, and we followed Zaven to ground transportation. He zipped us over to the Oakmont Apartments in Toluca Lake. The complex was older, but it was still one of the most popular temporary housing facilities in LA. We checked-in at the main office, and Sally greeted us with a smile. "I've got your unit all ready. If you'll give me just a moment, I'll get the paperwork for you to sign, then I'll take you over to the unit.

She returned shortly with a manila folder that contained a lease agreement. Scarlett signed on the dotted line, and Sally gave her a copy.

"No pets, right?" Sally asked.

"Right," Scarlett replied.

"The first and last month's rent has already been paid, along with the security deposit. You'll get the deposit back upon final inspection after move out."

She led us out of the office to a large golf cart. Zaven followed in the limo as Sally whisked us across the complex.

The sky was clear, and the temperature was 72°. It was a typical Southern California day.

"Each building has its own pool," Sally said. "There is a convenience store on site, along with a rental car company. The unit comes fully furnished with kitchen, microwave, cable TV, Internet, and an in-unit washer and dryer. You've got a one bedroom with a queen, and there is a pull-down Murphy bed in the living room for guests."

She parked the cart at building C.

I helped Zaven unload the bags.

"I've got it, sir."

He insisted, but it took two trips to get the heavy bags up the steps to unit #212.

"So, are you two like a couple?" Sally asked as we stood at the door.

"No," I said quickly.

Sally opened the door and motioned for us to enter. It was a cozy little apartment, and the balcony offered a nice view of the Hollywood Hills.

Scarlett's wide eyes soaked in her first apartment.

"This is amazing!"

"Are you an actress?" Sally asked, knowing the answer. Everyone in Hollywood that looked like Scarlett was an actress.

"Yes," Scarlett said, excitedly.

"You're conveniently located next to the studios, and we're not far from Griffith Park," Sally said. "We have lots of actors at the facility. Celebrities too. Sometimes they just like to escape and come here. And we are the number one facility for child actors that come out here during pilot season."

"Pilot season?" Scarlett asked.

"When they film all the new TV pilots that might go on to become TV shows."

"Oh, exciting."

"Here are your apartment keys and the remote to the entry gates. This is a parking permit that you must keep visible in your car if you are parking on the premises." Sally handed her a welcome packet with information about the property rules, local restaurants, shopping, etc. "Here's my card. Please don't hesitate to call me if you need anything. I hope you enjoy your stay."

With that, Sally left us to our own devices.

Zaven carted the baggage in from the hallway and lugged Scarlett's bags into her bedroom. When he returned to the living room, he said, "Once again, I'm yours for the day. I'll be waiting in the parking lot when you need me."

I thanked him, and Zaven pulled the door shut as he left the apartment.

Scarlett strolled around the unit, taking it all in. It smelled like fresh paint and pot-pourri. "This is so cool. Thank you for taking me out here. I think I would have been too scared to come by myself."

"You're welcome."

She slipped into the kitchen and pulled open the fridge. It was empty. "We need to go grocery shopping."

"Just order online."

"Good idea."

Scarlett dashed to her bags in the bedroom, pulled out a laptop, and returned. She set the computer on the kitchen counter and clacked away at the keys while I called Joel.

His receptionist answered. After a brief hold, Joel came on the line. "Are you here?"

"Yeah, we're getting situated in the apartment now."

"Great. Why don't you swing by the agency around 4 PM? Scarlett can see the office and meet my assistant. Then we can grab happy hour at the *Point*. It's just a block over. With traffic it should take you 45 minutes to get to Century City from the Valley."

I told Joel we'd see him soon and hung up.

Scarlett suddenly looked panicked. "We're meeting Joel at 4 PM?"

"Yeah, is that a problem?"

"What am I going to wear?"

I shrugged. "Something cute."

Scarlett shook her head. "Nope. Cute is not going to cut it. This is the first time I meeting him in person. I need to look *hot!*"

"I don't think Joel is susceptible to your charms."

"That means he has an even more discerning eye."

Scarlett rushed into the bedroom and began rummaging through her suitcases. She changed several times over the next 45 minutes, displaying different outfits, wanting my opinion. She looked great in all of them, and I told her so.

"You're not helping," Scarlett grumbled.

"What? They all look fine."

"We're not going for *fine*. We are going for *take your breath away, drop dead gorgeous, that girl is going to be a movie star.*"

I sighed. "You can't go wrong with a little black dress."

Her eyes lit up. "I have the perfect one."

She slipped back into the bedroom, then emerged a moment later with a dress that looked painted on. It had a low-cut neck, and a high hemline. The stiletto heels accented her toned legs. Her makeup was flawless.

"That's the one!"

"Are you sure you're not just saying that because you're tired of looking at dresses?"

"Would I lie to you?"

"No." She smiled. "Thank you, Tyson."

She spun around and sauntered back into the bedroom to

make some last-minute adjustments, then emerged a moment later, looking like a goddess.

We climbed into the posh limousine and Zaven drove us over the hill, into Hollywood. We cruised down Sunset Boulevard, and Scarlett marveled at the sites.

"It doesn't seem real." She said, gazing out the tinted windows. "I feel like I'm in the middle of a crazy dream and I'm going to wake up back in my bed."

"Let me give you a little piece of advice," I said. "You can't take anything at face value around here. It's all just talk until the check clears. Stay focused, keep striving for your goals, but take it all with a grain of salt."

"That's good advice."

"Don't get caught up in all the bullshit." I had no idea if she would listen to me. "Tomorrow the limousine will be gone. And Jack's only going to pay for that apartment for a few months. This is an opportunity, and you need to make the most of it."

She smiled. "I will. I promise."

Zaven turned down *Avenue of the Stars* and pulled the limousine around the circular drive to the entryway of the towering glass building that housed *Inventive Artists Agency,* the most powerful agency in Hollywood.

He parked the vehicle, hopped out, jogged around, and pulled open the door. Scarlett stepped out of the limousine like the movie star she was destined to be. I slid across the leather seats and stepped out behind her.

Zaven told me to call when we were heading back down so he could have the car ready.

Scarlett and I strolled through the glass double doors and greeted the receptionist at the desk. I told her who we were here to see, and she scanned the visitor list. Finding our names, she gave us two visitor badges and pointed to a bank of elevators.

Scarlett's eyes widened as Chloe-C strolled through the lobby—she was the biggest pop star in the galaxy.

13

Scarlett resisted the urge to ask for Chloe-C's autograph.

We made our way to the elevator bank and up to Joel's office on the 20th floor. It was the motion picture department. Floor to ceiling glass and sleek furniture decorated the area. Agents squawked on phones, and assistants scurried about in fear for their jobs. Interns hustled paperwork back and forth between offices.

This was where the magic *really* happened.

The studios may have held the purse strings, but the agents held the real power—access to talent. No Hollywood movie is complete without a blockbuster star. And to get that star, you need to go through the agent.

The agency represented writers, directors, cinematographers, actors, and producers. They put together complete packages—stuffed with all of their own talent—and pitched the studios on a regular basis.

We made our way through the chaos to Joel's office.

"Go right in," the receptionist said. "He's waiting."

We pushed through the double doors.

Joel greeted us with open arms and a wide smile. "I'm so glad you're finally here!"

He gave Scarlett a big hug.

"It's so nice to finally meet you," Scarlett said. "I can't thank you enough for everything you've done for me. This is a great opportunity, and I promise I won't disappoint."

"Well, Tyson speaks very highly of you. I tend to trust my talent when they make recommendations. I take it you had a good flight?"

Scarlett nodded.

"Excellent." Joel smiled. "Maybe one day you can have your own private jet?"

"That would be nice," Scarlett said.

Joel looked at his watch. "I don't know about you, but I'm ready for a drink. We can catch happy hour at the *Point*. It's just down the block. Great for people watching."

We left the agency and made a short walk to the old-school Hollywood bar with mahogany walls and an elegant atmosphere. The kind of place where people would smoke cigars and close deals if smoking wasn't banned. Black and white photos of movie stars from the '50s, '60s, and '70s lined the wall. Numerous agents and clients mixed and mingled, talking about projects, pitching ideas, plotting world domination.

We had gotten access to the inner sanctum of Hollywood powerbrokers. It felt like we were getting a glimpse of the illuminati. I was almost surprised we didn't see people in flowing black robes sacrificing goats.

There was no secret handshake to get in the door, but this was the kind of place that didn't let just *anybody* in. I'm sure there was a list, and the hostesses were trained to recognize the behind-the-scenes powerbrokers. If you lacked sufficient sway in town, you'd find a very cool reception at the hostess stand, and all the tables would be full.

The hostess looked like she could have been a model. Long dark hair straightened to perfection, high cheekbones, red lips. She sat us at a table not far from the bar, and a waitress stopped by to take our order.

"I'll have a martini," Joel said, then pointed at me. "And you're a *whiskey, rocks* guy, right?"

I nodded.

"And you?" Joel asked, pointing to Scarlett.

"Water for me," Scarlett said.

"Coming right up!" the waitress said. "Would you like any appetizers?"

"Bring us a sampler platter," Joel said.

The *Point* was connected to a posh hotel that had five star dining. They served Mediterranean-style cuisine with an array of wild-caught seafood. The waitress returned shortly with our drinks, and Joel got down to business.

"So, I've got you enrolled in classes with Easton Carter," Joel said. "He is a very respected acting coach, and there's a six month waiting list to get into class. But... I pulled some strings for you."

Scarlett smiled. "Thank you."

"Pay attention. Do everything he says. And don't skip out on class."

"I'm there. Whatever it takes."

"Good. I'm not going to send you out on any auditions until you're ready. You get one chance to make a first impression, and I'm not ruining either of our reputations. Got it?"

"Got it."

"Some people are quick studies," Joel said. "Others take years to master the craft."

Scarlett's face went long.

"Don't worry. You're a smart girl. I think you'll be a quick study. But I will keep in touch with Easton, and when he thinks you're ready, we'll be off to the races."

"Sounds like a plan!" she said with a smile.

"I don't know what your financial situation is, or if you need to get a job in the meantime, but stay out of trouble. It's really easy to fall in with the fast crowd around here, and the next thing you know, things are out of control."

"I've already been through my *out-of-control* phase. This is totally my *in control* phase."

"Let's hope so," Joel said.

"You can count on me," Scarlett assured.

"And I'm sure if money gets tight, uncle Tyson here can help you out." Joel patted me on the shoulder.

"I can help out for 15% of the gross," I said.

Joel laughed. "A man after my own heart." He turned his attention back to Scarlett. "So, do you have any questions for me?"

Scarlett thought about it for a moment. "What else do I need to be doing to make this *thing* happen?"

"I'm so glad you asked. Most actors expect me to do all the work. To tell you the truth, the majority of this is all on your shoulders. I make the deals, but I've got to have *something* to make the deals with. You follow?"

"I think so."

"There's only one reason studios pay insane amounts of money for movie stars to act in their movies…. to get people into the theaters, or to buy the movie on VOD or physical media. That's it. End of story.

"Ever wonder why a terrible actor is such a star? It's because people want to watch them. Now, there are a whole host of reasons why people want to watch an actor. Maybe they're good? Maybe they're beautiful? Maybe they're intriguing? It doesn't really matter *why*, as long as they watch. It's your job to make sure you are utterly watchable. And it's your job to bring an audience. So, if you haven't started already, begin cultivating a social media following. Build your brand. And while we're speaking of brands, decide what your name is going to be. Are you going to present yourself to the world as Scarlett Donovan? Or something else?

"I like *Scarlett*. It evokes a certain quality. I think you could stick with Donovan, or you could go another way entirely. It's totally up to you, but pick a stage name that you can live with for the rest of your career."

Scarlett pondered Joel's advice for a moment. "I'll think of something. And I just want to say thank you again for everything that you're doing for me. I know that you don't give this opportunity to many people."

"I don't," Joel said. "So, you really should be thanking this guy." Joel patted me on the shoulder again.

"Thank you, Tyson."

"My pleasure. The best thanks you can give me is hard work and dedication."

"I will give you that," Scarlett said. "You can bet on it."

"Now, you and I have business to discuss," Joel said to me. "Between you and me, I think the script for the Bree Taylor story doesn't totally suck. *But*, you may have some issues with it. My advice would be to fight for your convictions without being a complete fucking asshole about it. At the end of the day, it's their money and their movie and you sold it to them. It's important to be strong in this town, but not unmanageable. So, being a little bit of an asshole is okay... too much is no bueno."

"I think you know me well enough by now," I said. "I don't mince words, and I don't bullshit."

"And I think that is a huge advantage. You can be quite intimidating. *Use* that." Joel paused. "By the same token, I think we can do more business with the studio. I've been putting the bug in their ear, and they're warming up to the idea of this TV show. A Florida mystery series, loosely based on your life. I've got a meeting set up tomorrow. You'll go in and pitch the show plus a series of episodes."

"I don't have anything prepared."

"Of course you do. Fictionalize every case you've worked on. You can't make that shit up."

Scarlett's eyes widened as she saw someone enter the bar. "Holy shit! Is that—"

Joel craned his neck over his shoulder and looked across the bar at the striking gentleman who just passed the hostess stand. "Yes, indeed that is Chase Michaels."

He was the number one box office draw, voted the sexiest man of the year, and most eligible bachelor.

"Would you like to meet him?" Joel asked.

Scarlett's jaw dropped. "Seriously? You know him?"

"Honey, I know everybody." Joel twisted around and waved Chase over. "Chase!"

The movie star nodded to Joel and strolled our way.

Scarlett squirmed nervously. "Holy fucking shit," she muttered under her breath. "How do I look?"

"You look fine," I said. "Try not to act like a groupie."

Her eyes narrowed at me.

Chase had one of those TV heads—large, square jaw, brilliantly white teeth. He almost looked freakish in person. He strolled to the table, and Joel introduced us. Scarlett looked like she was about to have a heart attack.

"Scarlett is a new client at the agency," Joel said, proudly. "And Tyson is responsible for the Bree Taylor story."

"I can't wait to see it," Chase said. "Bree was a sweetheart."

"This is Scarlett's first day in Los Angeles," Joel added.

"Really? Welcome," Chase said.

"Thank you," Scarlett replied, staring up at him with awestruck eyes.

"Well, if you need someone to show you around town, I'm happy to do it."

Scarlett was speechless for a moment. She stammered, "Yes. Absolutely. That would be great. I mean, if I'm not too busy."

He chuckled at her sarcasm. "Joel has my number. Call me anytime."

"I will."

Chase smiled before leaving the table to meet his friends across the bar.

Scarlett leaned back in her chair and clutched her heart. "I think I can die now."

"Don't die just yet," Joel said. "At least wait till you've made a few movies."

"I want to have that man's babies," Scarlett said.

"You and every other aspiring actress in Hollywood," Joel said. "But hold off on the babies—"

"Until I make a few movies. I got it."

I rolled my eyes.

"And on another note, don't give *it* away too easy around here. I know some girls use their assets to work their way up the Hollywood ladder, but more often than not, it doesn't always work out as anticipated. And be *safe*. Everybody around here is screwing everybody." Joel leaned in and muttered. "And let me tell you, everybody has got *something*. But you didn't hear that from me."

Scarlett cringed.

Joel looked at his watch. "I've got to run. Dinner at the *Palm*. Feel free to stay here as long as you like. Put everything on my tab." Joel looked to me. "You've got a 10 AM tomorrow at the studio. Don't be late."

"You're not going?"

"Unlike my talent, I work for a living. I can't hold your hand every time. You know the drill. You'll be great." He smiled at Scarlett and extended his hand. "It was a pleasure, my dear. I look forward to great things."

Scarlett's eyes sparkled.

Joel left just as the waitress brought the appetizers. He grabbed a crab cake and stuffed it into his mouth before sauntering out of the bar.

"I can't believe this is my life," Scarlett said.

"Just try to balance things out. Not every day is going to be like this."

"But it could be," she said in singsong with a smile.

I happened to glance to the door as I chowed on a grilled shrimp. I grimaced at what I saw.

14

Reagan stood at the hostess stand with some guy.

"Hey, isn't that...?" Scarlett asked.

"Yup," I said.

"Did you tell her you were coming to Los Angeles?"

"No."

"Who do you think the dude is? New boyfriend?"

My eyes narrowed at Scarlett.

"Sensitive... Still not over her, huh?"

I didn't respond.

"She's coming this way," Scarlett muttered.

"Tyson? Is that you?" Reagan shouted, strutting toward me.

I stood up, and she gave me one of those casual hugs.

"What are you doing here?"

"I have a few meetings, and Scarlett has a new agent."

Reagan smiled at Scarlett. "Impressive."

The dude she was with hovered nearby, looking awkward.

Reagan stammered uncomfortably, "Oh, this is my... boyfriend... Dylan. Dylan this is Tyson Wild and Scarlett Donovan."

I did my best to hide my disdain as I shook the man's hand.

"Dylan is a producer," Reagan said, filling the awkward silence.

Nobody said anything.

"Well, it was good to see you," Reagan said. "You should have let me know you were coming in town. We could have done... lunch."

I shrugged. "Quick trip."

"Scarlett, are you living here now?"

She nodded.

"Well, if you need anything, you've got my number," Reagan said.

"Thanks," Scarlett replied.

The new boyfriend dragged Reagan away to their table. Reagan kept looking over her shoulder at me.

"New boyfriend, huh? That was quick," Scarlett said, snidely.

I played it off. "She doesn't owe me anything."

"Yeah, but still."

I flagged the waitress down and told her to put our bill on Joel's tab. We made short work of the appetizers and got out of there quickly.

We walked down the sidewalk back to the agency. I called Zaven and let him know we'd be there shortly. Scarlett took in the skyline of Century City. She pointed at a building. "Isn't that the building they used in *Die Hard?*"

"It is. Isn't that movie a little before your time?"

She gasped. "Best Christmas movie ever!"

I had to agree.

We reached the agency and climbed into the back of the limousine. Zaven drove us back to the Valley, and we got a taste of LA traffic at its finest—but sitting in the back of a limousine during rush hour wasn't so bad, especially with a stocked bar.

"You need to call Jack and let him know we got here okay."

"I sent him a text earlier," Scarlett replied.

"Well, check in with him from time to time so he doesn't worry."

"Jack? Worry?"

"About you? More than you think."

Zaven dropped us off at the Oakmont, and I cut him loose for the evening. He said he'd pick me up in the morning to take me to breakfast and the studio. I said 8 AM would be fine.

Scarlett still had a look of wonder in her eyes when she strolled into the apartment. "I can't believe this is mine."

"For the next few months, at least."

"It will be longer than that. I promise you. I'm not going home a failure." She paused. "You should have kept the limo. We could have partied tonight?"

I gave her a stern look.

"And when I say party, I mean we could hit the bars on Sunset. You could drink, and I could watch you drink. I would be the designated sober person to keep you out of trouble."

I rolled my eyes. "Keep *me* out of trouble? That's rich. And you're not supposed to frequent bars while you're on probation."

"Who will know?"

"If you get arrested in a bar out here, your probation officer will know."

"Easy." Scarlett smiled. "I just don't get arrested."

My scowl persisted.

"Fine," she sighed. "I'll just continue leading the same boring life that I have been leading back in Coconut Key."

"Good. With all this spare time, you can focus on your acting."

Scarlett's phone dinged with a text message. Her eyes sparkled, and she bounced up and down. She looked like she was about to explode. "Oh my God! *He's* texting me!"

"Who?"

"He got my number from Joel." Scarlett spun the phone around and showed me the display.

It was a text message from Chase.

Just as quickly as she showed me the screen, she snatched it back to read the text message again. "He wants me to meet him at *Star Bar!*"

"I don't think that's such a good idea," I said.

"Don't be such a party pooper! It's *Chase Michaels*. Do you really expect me not to go?"

"Come on. You know exactly what he wants."

Scarlett smiled. "And I expect to give it to him."

I arched an eyebrow at her.

"I'm kidding. Sort of. Not really." Scarlett planted her hands firmly on her hips. "I am a woman with needs. And, my God, he's Chase Michaels!"

I raised my hands in surrender. "It's none of my business."

"It's not like I'm going to get any sitting around here," she said, her eyes blazing into me, pointedly. "Lord knows I've tried." She sighed. "I'm not going to drink or do drugs or anything that could screw up my probation."

"Except for illegally entering a bar. How are you going to get in?"

"Look at me. I'm smoking hot. Who's going to turn me down? I'll be with one of the most famous movie stars in the world. I think he could pull a few strings." She paused. "Do NOT tell Jack."

"I'm staying out of this."

Scarlett scheduled an Uber. A few moments later, she got a notification that the driver had arrived. She gave me a hug and kissed me on the cheek. "Don't worry. I'll be fine."

With that, she was out the door.

Jack was going to kill me.

15

The morning sun blazed through the blinds, painting a pattern across the Murphy bed. I never heard Scarlett come home last night, and I was beginning to get concerned. I climbed out of bed and staggered to her bedroom door which was wide open. The sheets had been untouched, and her clothes were still scattered about the room from when she tried them all on last night.

I sent her a text message: [Are you okay?]

There was no immediate reply.

I took a shower, got dressed, then called Zaven. He picked me up and drove me to Bob's diner for breakfast. I had enough time to shovel a plate of scrambled eggs in my mouth, then get over to the studio for my meeting. We drove onto the lot and stopped at the security gate. The guard checked the list, then gave Zaven a pass.

The limousine cruised past mammoth soundstages to the

executive offices. Zaven pulled to the curb, hopped out, and got my door. "Break a leg!"

"Thanks."

I strolled into the building and found Susan's office. Her assistant greeted me with a smile. "Susan will be with you shortly. Can I get you anything? Water, juice, tea?"

I remembered Joel's advice to always take a bottle of water into a pitch meeting. I didn't anticipate getting nervous—I didn't *get* nervous about this type of thing. "Water, please."

"Certainly, Mr. Wild."

I was surprised she remembered my name. I took a seat on the sofa in the reception area and waited a few minutes.

The assistant returned a moment later with bottled water then took a seat behind her desk. She answered calls and clacked on the keyboard. She was a pretty girl. Raven black hair, short bangs cut in the shoulder-length bob. I wondered if she was secretly an actress, or an aspiring writer? Everyone had aspirations in this town.

A few minutes later, she said, "Susan will see you now."

I stood up and strolled toward Susan's office, and the assistant held the door for me.

"Tyson, it's so good to see you again!" Susan said with a beaming smile.

She was one of the most powerful women in Hollywood. The gatekeeper. The one who could launch or destroy careers. She was always warm and friendly to me, but I got the impression that if you got on her bad side, you might never work again in this town.

She gave me a hug and an air kiss. "I am so excited about the script for the Bree Taylor project. I hope you are too. Have you had a chance to read it?"

"I have. Joel gave me a copy."

"And... What did you think?"

I took a deep breath.

Susan motioned for us to take a seat on the sofa. There was a central desk with a computer, two opposing couches with a coffee table in between, and a large flatscreen display. Susan had access to every motion picture created by the studio, and their competitors. She could bring up films, trailers, and other promotional materials at the click of a button.

"I can give you my thoughts, if you want to hear them, or I can smile and tell you the script is great as is?" I said.

"I'd like to hear your honest reaction."

I hesitated a moment. Did honest actually *mean* honest? This was Hollywood after all.

"I liked the script," I said. I knew better than to go straight to the bad news. I always liked to start on a positive note, give my feedback, then finish positive. "But there were a few areas that... need some work."

Susan arched a curious eyebrow.

"There are some factual inconsistencies and several scenes that are complete fabrications. And there are some incorrect things from a technical standpoint."

"Keep in mind we will need to take some dramatic license to create suspense and manage the pacing."

"I understand."

I proceeded to give her detailed notes, then finished strong. "Overall, I think it's a fabulous script and a compelling story."

"I value your input. These are keen observations. I will pass them along to the writers and the director. This is the first draft. It's a long process, and the script will go through several iterations before it hits the screen."

"At the end of the day, it's your show," I said. "You know what you're doing. I trust you."

As long as the studio kept writing big checks, I wasn't going to put up too much of a fight. I just wanted to make sure that Bree's memory was respected, and that I didn't come off looking like an idiot.

We talked about a television series based on the happenings around Coconut Key. I told her about the *Sandcastle Killer,* and she seemed intrigued.

The meeting lasted about 45 minutes. Susan thanked me for my time, and I told her it was nice to see her again.

I had turned my phone on silent during the meeting, and a few text messages had buzzed my pocket. I swiped my screen anxiously as I walked through the hallways of the executive offices.

A text message from Scarlett read: *[Just got home. How did your meeting go?]*

[Fine. Heading back to the apartment now.]

Zaven drove me back to Oakmont. I told myself I wasn't going to ask about her evening, but the question slipped from my lips as I entered the apartment. "So, how did it go last night?"

"It was so cool. He's a really nice guy. I thought he might be totally full of himself, but he was really down to earth. He said he would help me with my career." She paused. "And no, I didn't sleep with him if that's what you're wondering?"

I raised my hands, innocently. "None of my business."

"We hung out at the bar, I met a bunch of his friends. We danced, then we went back to his place for an after party. I got tired early and crashed in one of the spare bedrooms."

"I'm glad you had a good time."

Jack called, and I was glad that Scarlett was back at the apartment. I didn't know what I would have said to him if I hadn't heard from her.

"I hate to cut your trip short, but you need to get back to Coconut Key," Jack said.

"What's going on?"

16

"Porter was picked up in a stolen car," Jack said. "Daniels has him in a holding cell."

"So, what's the urgency?" I asked. "We've got more than enough evidence to make a case."

"I'm not so sure about that."

"What do you mean?"

"I'll let you talk to him and see for yourself."

"His prints were on the door," I exclaimed. "If that's not damning evidence—"

"I'm not saying he wasn't there. I just think this guy might walk, and we may need to be looking at other suspects."

I sighed. "I'll be on a plane this afternoon."

"How's things with the miscreant?"

"She's all settled. Do you want to talk to her? She's right here."

I handed my phone to Scarlett.

"Hey Jack," Scarlett said.

I could barely hear JD's voice crackle through the tiny speaker.

"Yeah. The apartment's great. Everything's fine."

Jack mumbled something.

"Yes, I'm behaving myself." Scarlett glanced to me and pressed her fingers to her full lips, urging me to keep my mouth shut.

They chitchatted for a few minutes, then Scarlett handed the phone back to me. JD had already hung up, so I slipped the phone in my pocket.

"Are you really going back today?" Scarlett asked.

I nodded.

"But... But..." She made a pouty face. "I'm gonna be all alone."

"Goes with the territory."

Scarlett frowned. It was just starting to hit her that, for the first time in her life, she was on her own. *Mostly*.

Her eyes misted, and she gave me a hug. "Thanks for taking me out here. I'm going to miss you and Jack."

"We'll miss you too."

She sneered at me. "No, you won't."

"I'm sure I'll be back before too long with this movie stuff."

She smiled. "Yay!"

I made arrangements for the private jet, packed my bags, called Zaven, and said my final goodbyes. Scarlett's eyes misted again.

"The next time I see you, you're going to have a part in a movie, or a TV show."

She wiped her eyes and smiled. "Damn straight!"

I lugged my bag down the steps to the parking lot, and Zaven threw it in the trunk of the limousine. I slipped into the back, and he zipped me to the FBO at the Burbank airport.

I was back in Coconut Key just as the sun vanished over the horizon.

Jack picked me up in the lizard green Porsche, and I stuffed my roller case under the hood (since the engine was in the rear). It barely fit. It wasn't a car designed for excess storage, and unlike his older cabriolet, this speedster didn't have a backseat. There was no practicality to the car. It had one purpose, and one purpose only.

"We have a little problem," Jack shouted over the roar of the engine as we zipped out of the airport.

The night air ruffled my hair, and the breeze was cool.

"Our power couple, Brad and Brandi, are on video, trying to break into a pet grooming salon from 9 to 10 PM. Brenda is adamant that Warren's death occurred within that window."

"So? Brad goes over to the house sometime beforehand, beats Warren. The old man lay helpless on the floor for a few hours, then finally dies. I don't think that video exonerates them."

The development irritated me. I was pretty sure we had our suspect, now that theory was on shaky ground.

"Why? Why try to rob a pet store after killing Warren?"

"Maybe Brad didn't find any money in the house? They needed a fix. They attempted to rob a pet store."

Jack drove to the Sheriff's Office.

I ripped into Brad Porter in an interrogation room. He sat at a table, handcuffed. The overhead florescent lights flickered and buzzed. "Just do us all a favor. Tell me the truth."

"I am telling you the truth," Porter growled.

"Bullshit."

"I'm telling you, man. I didn't kill the guy!" Brad exclaimed. "I mean, you got me on video for B&E. What more do you want?"

"I want you to tell me that you beat a helpless old man and he died."

Porter sighed. "Okay, fine. It wasn't one of my better moments. But I'm telling you, I didn't kill him. Yes, I went over to that house to get some money. Brandi told me the old man always kept cash around. Didn't trust banks. She said the guy had money stuck in coat pockets, sock drawers, old shoes. But I'll tell you... I didn't find shit, and I tore through everything."

"And that's when you killed him?"

Porter shook his head. "No, man! Get the dog shit out of

your ears. I punched the guy once. *Once!* That was it. He fell down, but he was conscious when I left."

I glared at the scumbag. "You hit a 92-year-old man! What the fuck is wrong with you?"

"I got a problem. Okay. I admit it. Are you happy now?"

I scowled at the dirtbag. My fists clenched, and I wanted to beat him to a pulp, but I restrained myself.

"I was broke, and I needed money for drugs. Is that what you want me to say?"

"Just because he was breathing when you left him, doesn't mean that the damage you inflicted didn't kill him."

"No. No way! I didn't hit him that hard."

"He was 92!" I shouted. "You didn't have to hit him *that* hard."

"You not pinning murder on me, pal."

"I'm not your pal," I barked.

My face twisted with disgust. I left the interrogation room before my emotions got the better of me. I joined JD, Sheriff Daniels, and Brenda in the hallway. "He's sticking with the story that he just hit Warren once."

"The guy's a scumbag, but I don't think he's our killer," Daniels said. "The pharmacist at the drug store says he saw Warren in there about 8:30 PM on the night of his death. The security footage corroborates this. The pharmacist said Warren had a bruise on his face and a laceration on his cheek. He bought butterfly strips to close the wound. Warren said he had fallen. The pharmacist urged him to go to the hospital to get checked out, but Warren refused. Said he was *fine*."

I clenched my jaw and grumbled to myself.

"I feel the same way you do," Daniels said. "I wanted this to be the guy. But it's not. So go find out who is."

17

Despite being Wednesday night, there was a decent crowd and lots of eye-candy sauntering around. JD and I reclined on lounge chairs by the pool, watching wet fabric cling to curvaceous bodies. Fit, beautiful people frolicked around the water. We had stopped by to see Jack's favorite waitress, Harper, at the outdoor bar at *Tide Pool.*

Jack hadn't mentioned anything about Scarlett yet, but I could tell it was on his mind. He was midway through his drink when he finally asked, "How do you think Scarlett is adjusting?"

"I think she's adjusting fine."

"That almost worries me. I just don't want her to fall in with the wrong crowd and revert to her old ways."

I shared the same concerns. "There comes a time where everybody has to stand or fall on their own."

Jack sighed, then took a sip of his whiskey. His eyes took in the smorgasbord of visual delights. Toned girls in *barely there* bikinis sauntered around the pool, jiggling in the most sublime of ways. Drinks flowed, and music boomed.

"It looks like we're back to square one," Jack said. "Any ideas?"

"Mrs. Grant said Warren volunteered at a nursing home. I think we should pay a visit tomorrow. Ask around."

Jack looked at me like I was crazy. "What? Do you think somebody at the nursing home beat him to death?"

"No, but it might give us more insight into his daily life."

"He was probably diddling a few of those old ladies," Jack said. "Seemed like Warren got around."

"Maybe a jealous husband decided to put a stop to his philandering?" I suggested.

Jack rolled his eyes. "You think one of those old men at the nursing home really went after Warren?" he asked in an incredulous tone. "Beat him senseless?"

"I guess we'll see, won't we?"

Jack dismissed the notion entirely. "That's a pretty heavy beating for a senior citizen to administer, don't you think?"

"You've got an AARP card, don't you?" I couldn't resist the urge to give him shit.

"Fuck you!" Jack sneered at me. "And I might give you a beat down if you're not careful."

We spent the rest of the evening lounging at *Tide Pool,* taking in the sights. The next day, we headed over to the *Coconut Key Assisted Living Facility.* It was both a skilled nursing facility and an assisted living complex. There were two distinct wings, depending on the need of care. It overlooked the water and had a private beach. The receptionist at the front desk greeted us with a smile. "How can I help you gentlemen?"

Audrey had dark curly hair, a round face, and square glasses.

JD flashed his badge. "We'd like to talk to you about Warren Russell."

A grim look washed over her face. "I heard about what happened. That's just terrible!"

"We were told that he volunteered around the facility," I said.

Audrey nodded. "I think he was here almost every day. When he didn't show up, I thought the worst."

"Can you think of anyone who might have wanted to do Warren harm?" I asked.

"Oh, God no! Everybody loved Warren."

"I heard he was quite the ladies' man," JD said.

"He certainly was a charmer," the receptionist said with a grin.

"Do you think his charm could have caused issues for him?" I asked.

She looked surprised. "Oh, I think I know what you mean." She paused a moment, then looked around the lobby before speaking. In a hushed tone, she said, "I don't like to gossip, but... there were more than a few angry husbands."

I glanced to JD with a cocky grin on my face.

He rolled his eyes.

"Anybody make any threats?" I asked.

"Eugene confronted him one day. Right in the lounge area. He took his cane and swung it at Warren, and damn near fell over in the process. One of the nurses broke it up before things got out of hand."

"Do you think Eugene could have been responsible for Warren's death?"

"No. No way. He's just not physically capable."

"He could have hired somebody," I said.

"Eugene's all talk. He would never do something like that."

"Is he around?" I asked. Do you think we might be able to talk to him?"

Audrey hesitated. "Sure. Let me call Todd. He can show you to Eugene's unit."

She picked up the phone and dialed an extension. "Todd, can you come to the front desk? There are two gentlemen here with the County Sheriff's Department. They'd like to speak with Eugene." She paused, listening. "Okay, great. I'll tell them." She hung up the phone. "Todd will be with you shortly."

"Can you give me a list of the women that Warren had relationships with?" I asked.

"Well, I don't think that information is protected by HIPAA." Her eyes shifted, and her face scrunched, as she thought about it. "Well, there was Rosemary, Deborah, Betty,

Kathryn, Maggie, Margaret, Shanice, Elizabeth, Hilda, Judy..."

JD and I exchanged a glance.

"I can make a full list if you want me to. He was pretty popular."

"I see," JD said.

About that time, Todd strolled around the corner. He was a tall, thin guy with a salesman's smile and short brown hair. He wore a suit and tie and was clearly part of administration. He extended his hand and introduced himself. "I'm the owner and general manager of C-KALF, as we like to call it." He muttered aside, "It can get a little slow around here sometimes, so we call it *Decaf,* if you get my drift. I can take you to Eugene's unit. He's currently in the assisted living section of our facility. He's a little mobility challenged at the moment."

"What happened?"

"Just had a knee replacement."

"When?" I asked.

"Last week, I think. I can get the exact date for you, if you need it."

We followed Todd down the hallway which smelled like moth balls, cleaning supplies, urine, and stale baloney. It all swirled around and mixed together, creating a unique aroma.

The facility looked clean and well-maintained, but the pale green walls and overhead florescent lights made it feel more like a hospital than a place you'd want to spend your golden years. The whole thing gave me the willies. Watching frail people shuffle down the hallways, clinging to creaky walkers—with bright yellow tennis balls on the legs—was hard to swallow. It brought me face to face with my own mortality.

I did NOT want to end up in one of these places. I kept reassuring myself that I wouldn't last that long. Somewhere out there was a bullet with my name on it. I was sure of it. Maybe that would be my salvation from old age?

We reached Eugene's room near the end of the hallway. His door was open, and the TV flickered, mounted on the wall. Eugene was at the edge of his bed, gripping his walker, preparing to stand.

Todd rushed to his aid. "Now, you know better than this, Eugene. You're a fall risk, and you're supposed to have supervision when you're moving about the room."

"Your mother's a fall risk," Eugene quipped. "I gotta take a leak."

"It's for your own safety," Todd said.

"I can make it to the bathroom on my own!" Eugene insisted.

"I'm sure you can. I'll call for the nurse, just to be on the safe side."

Eugene grumbled to himself.

"You have some visitors," Todd said in a cheery voice. "They'd like to ask you a few questions."

Eugene glanced toward us as we hovered in the doorway. A scowl twisted on his face. "Who the fuck are they?"

Todd smiled. "They're deputies with the Sheriff's Department."

"Oh, good. I'd like to make a complaint about this asshole," Eugene said, pointing to Todd.

Todd forced an awkward smile. "I don't think Eugene likes some of my rules."

"I don't like you." Eugene didn't mince words. He was at that age where he just didn't care. If he ever had a filter, it had worn out. "And I don't like some of the food you serve around here. Tuesday is hamburger day. And I don't know where they get those patties from, but I have a sneaking suspicion it ain't hamburger. And some of those young harlots are cheating on bingo. I guarantee it."

"Nobody's cheating on bingo," Todd assured. "And the hamburger is indeed 100%, Grade A beef."

"Well, they taste like dog turds."

"Mr. Whittaker, we can discuss all this later," Todd said. "But these deputies have much more important things to talk about, and their time is valuable."

JD muttered in my ear, "Still think this guy did it?"

"Mr. Whittaker, do you know Warren Russell?" I asked.

His face twisted, and he groaned. "You tell that slimy son-of-a-bitch that next time I see him, I'm gonna shove this walker up his ass."

"I'd tell him, but he's dead."

Eugene lifted his brow. "You don't say?"

"You wouldn't happen to know anything about his demise, would you?" I asked.

"Can't say that I do."

"Seems like you were pretty upset with him," I said. "I heard that you threatened to kill him."

"Goddamn right I did! He was sticking his pickle where it didn't belong. I don't know where you come from, son, but in my world, that's grounds for an ass-whooping."

"So, he was having an affair with your wife?" I asked.

Eugene glowered at me. "What did I just say?"

"Did you do anything about it?" I asked.

"I tried, but they broke it up just as I was about to put a hurting on him."

"Ever think about hiring someone to do the job?" JD asked.

Eugene's face crinkled up. "Hell no. That's chickenshit. If a man can't take care of his own business, that's on him." He paused. "As soon as my knee was healed, I was going to go beat his ass."

A doctor entered the room wearing a white lab coat and a stethoscope around his neck. He had short dark hair, brown eyes, tan skin, and a square jaw. Dr. Gardner looked to be in his late 30s and had a bright, perfect smile. "And how are we doing this morning, Mr. Whitaker?"

"I'm still alive."

"That's better than the alternative," the handsome young doctor said.

"If you say so."

"Have you been working on your range of motion?" Gardner asked.

"I do what they tell me to do in PT."

"Let's have a look."

"If you bend my knee in a direction it doesn't want to go, I will kick your ass."

Gardner chuckled. "Careful now. I study mixed martial arts and Brazilian jujitsu."

Eugene scowled at him. "Yeah, well I was a helluva boxer in my day."

The good doctor smiled. "I bet you were. Now lets have a look at that knee."

JD muttered in my ear, "Come on. Let's go track down more octogenarian suspects."

I frowned at him.

We stepped into the hallway with Todd.

"Mr. Whitaker can be a handful at times, but I don't think he's who you are looking for," Todd said. "It's really tragic what happened to Warren Russell, but I don't think any of our residents are responsible. But I am happy to let you speak to as many as you need."

"I'd like to speak with Mr. Whitaker's wife,"

Todd cringed. "Mrs. Whitaker passed away a year ago. Sometimes Eugene forgets that."

We talked to a few of Warren's companions, and they all pretty much said the same thing. They raved about how kind he was, and how they would miss him. Each woman had their own theory as to who committed the crime. Most were preposterous theories, cribbed from detective shows. One woman even suggested a government conspiracy.

We thanked Todd for showing us around.

"My pleasure," he said. "If there's anything else you need, or have additional questions, please don't hesitate to contact me. I really do hope you find the person responsible. Something like this is truly unsettling."

We strolled out of the retirement home into the parking lot. It felt like we had escaped. I couldn't imagine having to live there full time.

"Mrs. Grant said Warren volunteered as a crossing guard. Maybe we should head to the middle school, talk to a few teachers and the principal?" I suggested.

JD's face twisted. "Oh, so now you think some 6th-grader beat him to death?"

My eyes narrowed at him.

18

"Deputy Wild?" a soft female voice said, crackling through the speaker in my phone.

I could barely hear her over the howl of the engine and the whistling of the wind as we barreled down the highway on our way to the middle school.

"Yes," I shouted over the noise. "How can I help you?"

"My name is Haley Russell. Warren was my grandfather. Sheriff Daniels gave me your number."

"I'm so sorry for your loss."

"Thank you. He said you and your partner were investigating the case."

"That's correct."

"I just wanted to make contact. If there is anything I can do to help your investigation, please let me know." She paused. "How is it going?"

"Right now we don't have anything promising. I'm sorry. But I can assure you, we will follow this through to conclusion."

"Thank you. I appreciate that. Warren's viewing is tonight at the *Serenity Harbor Funeral Home*, if you would like to attend. The funeral is scheduled for noon tomorrow. I'll be in town for the week, trying to wrap up my grandfather's affairs. I hope we can at least meet before I leave town."

"My partner and I will definitely attend either the viewing or the service. Again, I am sorry for your loss. Please don't hesitate to contact me if you have any questions."

"Thank you."

We pulled into the parking lot of the Coconut Key Middle School about the time the phone call ended. JD parked the Porsche in the faculty lot, and we strolled toward the main office. A bell rang, and a horde of school kids swarmed the hallways, heading toward their next class.

"Look at all these potential killers," JD teased.

We stepped into the main office and flashed our badges.

"Uh, oh!" the woman behind the front desk exclaimed as she saw us. Her wide eyes took in the glimmering badges. She was a frumpy woman with dark curly hair, and an acetate name tag that read *Dorothy*. "You haven't received any threats against the school, have you?"

"No, ma'am," I said. "Nothing like that."

I told her why we were there.

"Oh, thank God! I thought you were gonna tell me there was a bomb in a trashcan."

"No, ma'am."

The principal, Mr. Strickler, stepped out of his office just as I was explaining things to Dorothy. He introduced himself and expressed his condolences. "I thought you guys had pretty much settled on a suspect?"

"Didn't pan out as we hoped," I said.

"I'm sorry to hear that. Warren was here every day, rain or shine, always looking out for the kids," Strickler said.

"Did he have conflicts with anyone? Parents? Teachers? I hate to ask, but was he ever accused of any inappropriate behavior?"

Principal Strickler's face crinkled. "No. Not at all. Everybody loved Warren. He was a standup guy. Nothing inappropriate. I can tell you, if a parent would have raised a concern like that, he'd been out, lickety-split."

"Seems like he got along with just about everybody," I said. "Warren didn't have any *affairs* with any of the teachers, did he?"

"He was 92 years old," Strickler said, looking at me like I was crazy.

"Well, in our investigation, we've discovered that Warren was a bit of a ladies' man."

Strickler pondered things for a moment. "Well, he *was* an attractive man for his age. But I haven't heard any gossip about any tawdry affairs, have you, Dorothy?"

Dorothy shook her head.

"I don't know what to tell you," Strickler continued. "The

only people that didn't like Warren Russell, as far as I know, were the drug dealers on the street corners."

That statement piqued our interests.

"Drug dealers?" I asked.

"He'd run anybody off that was loitering around school premises that didn't belong," Strickler said.

"So, he got into confrontations with these dealers?" I asked.

"Warren wasn't scared to give a piece of his mind to anyone." Strickler thought about it for a moment. "A lot of times, we get older kids lingering around campus that are trying to recruit new users. It's disgusting. But, they start young sometimes." He paused. "Hell, if you go outside right now, I guarantee you there will be someone on the next block trying to hustle drugs to these kids on their way home from school."

"How long has this kind of thing been going on?" JD asked.

"It's endemic. Where you have kids, you will have drugs, and someone trying to sell to them. The best we can do is call you boys when we hear about it," Strickler said. "These dealers are clever. They are school-age, they wear backpacks and carry books. They try to blend in as much as possible."

"Thank you," I said. "This has been helpful."

"My pleasure," Strickler said as we shook hands. "If there's anything else I can do, let me know."

"Do you think you would recognize these street dealers?"

"I wouldn't, but Marcy might. She's another one of our volunteer crossing guards. She'll be here this afternoon. Talk to her."

We left the office and strolled through the halls toward the front of the main building.

"Are you thinking what I'm thinking?" JD asked.

"It sounds like somebody may have retaliated against Warren," I said.

We pushed through the glass double doors, descended the steps, and stood on the walkway. I gazed over the front lawn. The American flag fluttered high overhead, clinking against the flagpole. There was a large circular drive where parents picked up their children. At the south side of the school, the buses picked up and dropped off kids. Others walked home or rode their bikes.

JD and I decided to hang around until school let out. I called Denise in the meantime to see what kind of reports were on file about dealers around the school.

19

"It looks like we've received several complaints from school officials this year already. And we're what, not even six weeks into the school year?" Denise said.

"And what has been the outcome?" I asked.

"Records show we dispatched a unit to investigate the complaints. No arrests were made."

"That's it?"

"That's it," Denise said. She changed direction. "I'm really sorry about my friend getting out of control the other day. I hope you won't hold it against me."

"No worries." I paused. "I'd invite you back aboard, but since we are keeping things strictly *professional*, they'll be no more leisurely outings for you," I teased.

"I think it's for the best. Besides, I like our friendship, it would be a shame to ruin it over meaningless sex."

"Who said it would be meaningless?"

"Please, Tyson. Don't go there. I know better."

"I'll have you know that every woman I've been with has meant something," I said, making a pathetic attempt to defend my reputation.

"Yeah, I'm sure they meant a lot in the moment," she snarked.

"Well, when you think about it in a philosophical sense... all we really have is the present moment. The past is a memory, the future is but a dream."

I could almost hear her roll her eyes. "Okay, Aristotle, I will talk to you later."

Long before the dismissal bell rang, cars pulled into the circular drive. The traffic stacked up, and the line of metal twisted around the block. Students burst out of the doors and launched across the campus. It was pure chaos. Faces filled with jubilation, escaping the educational prison.

We talked to Marcy at the main crosswalk. She wore a lime green vest that was even brighter than JD's Porsche. She was in her late 50s, and her short, curly hair was just starting to go gray. We asked about Russell as she escorted the kids across the street.

"Yeah, Warren kept getting into it with this one kid. He ran him off a few times. I know for a fact the kid had a gun in his waistband one time Warren talked to him. But that didn't seem to scare Warren," Marcy said.

"How old was the kid?" I asked.

"I don't know. 16? Maybe 17?"

"Do you think you'd recognize him again if you saw him?"

"If he came around here? Sure. If you put him in a lineup, probably not."

"Do you think you could give a description to our sketch artist?" I asked.

"Sure. I'd be happy to do that."

We kept our eye out for anyone who looked suspicious. Jack and I walked around the campus and canvassed the nearby streets.

Nobody looked out of place.

After Marcy had finished her obligations at the school, she followed us down to the station and worked with Lana to come up with a sketch of the young drug dealer. She said the kid wore baggy jeans, colorful shirts, new shoes, and carried a backpack with *USA* in red, white, and blue across the top, and a large American Eagle embroidered on the fabric. We also showed her several mugshots of kids that had been arrested recently for possession or intent to distribute.

Marcy wasn't able to identify anyone.

By the time we wrapped up with Marcy, Warren's visitation was beginning. We headed to the *Serenity Harbor Funeral Home*. It was one of the last of the independent, privately owned aftercare facilities. Most had been snapped up by larger conglomerates. It was still a mom-and-pop shop. They did all of the embalming and body preparation in-house, unlike the larger corporations that sent remains to a central processing facility. They offered traditional burial, cremation, burial at sea, and spreading of the ashes at sea, if so desired. They had a relationship with the *Coconut Key Memorial Cemetery,* and offered discounts on plots and internment. None of it was cheap.

The parking lot was half full.

Haley greeted guests as they entered. She was a cute, sandy blonde with brown hair and soft skin. Her eyes were red and puffy from all the tears that had been shed, but she seemed to be holding up relatively well at the moment. She reached out and shook my hand and introduced herself. "You must be Tyson."

"How did you know?"

"You're under 65," she said, dryly.

All the attendees were older. There were some neighbors, a few women from the nursing home, and a few of Warren's acquaintances.

I introduced Haley to Jack.

"It's a pleasure to meet you. My condolences," JD said.

"I'm so glad you both could come," Haley said. "I wasn't sure who would show up, honestly. All of grandpa's Marine buddies have passed on. I tried to contact as many people as I could from Pappy's address book, but half of them were no longer with us."

"I guess that's the trouble with living to 92," Jack said. "You get to watch all of your friends and loved ones go first."

Haley frowned.

"I'm sorry," Jack said. "That was probably an inappropriate comment."

"You have to excuse Jack," I said. "He has no filter."

"I'm not offended. It's true. My grandfather lived a rich, full life. I'm sad that he's gone, and the way he went was tragic. But I refuse to let it bring me down. Instead, I'm going to be thankful of all the time that I had with him while he was alive."

"You have a good attitude," I said.

"Attitude is the only thing that you really control, isn't it?" Haley said.

I nodded.

"Besides, I know that you two capable gentlemen will bring his killer to justice."

"You can count on us," Jack said.

"Come on in, pay your respects and enjoy the refreshments," Haley said. "There is water, soda, and snacks. I'm paying for it, so you people better eat it."

We chuckled, then continued into the funeral home. We made our way to the viewing area where people viewed Warren peacefully resting in the casket. The makeup artist did a hell of a job. I never saw Warren when he was alive, but I knew how bad he looked when we arrived on scene. Now, his skin looked flawless and vibrant. Most of the time when you see a corpse in a funeral home they look overdone—thick makeup and too much blush. There is something unnatural about their appearance. But whoever did this make up had mastered their craft. He looked like he could sit up and climb out of the coffin at any moment.

There were long faces among the guests, but most people

tried to keep an upbeat attitude. After all, Warren had lived longer than most. In the US, life expectancy for men is 78.69 years. Warren had beaten that by 14 years. He probably had another half dozen in him if some scumbag hadn't taken that away.

We paid our respects, then we made our way to the refreshments.

"I don't know about you, but this shit is depressing," JD muttered. "I need a drink."

"So do I," Haley said, who happened to be in earshot.

20

Jack picked *Wetsuit* because their happy hour lasted till 8 PM.

That wasn't the only reason he picked the dive-themed bar. Gorgeous waitresses pranced around in wetsuit jackets unzipped to their navels. They looked like sexy super heroes of the deep. Bountiful cleavage practically spilled out of the formfitting neoprene. There were aquariums throughout the bar, filled with exotic fish. The walls were painted in a giant mural of the reefs. The drinks were strong, the music was good, and there was plenty of eye candy.

"I've just been so overwhelmed the last few days," Haley said. "It's good to get out and unwind. I've been going through all the things in Pappy's house, deciding what to keep, and what to throw away. It makes me dizzy. And I break down crying every 15 minutes. There are so many pictures, and so many memories. There are boxes and boxes of papers. He kept everything."

Jack and I listened to her with somber faces.

"I'm sorry. I don't mean to bore you with this," Haley said. "I didn't come out with you guys to complain."

"No problem. Gotta get it out. You hold that inside, it can turn rotten," I said.

The table was silent for a moment.

"You guys don't seem like your average cops," she said with a curious look in her eyes.

"You're not going to find anything average here," JD said with a smile.

"We volunteer at the department and assist with special cases," I said.

"I'm glad my grandfather's case is special," Haley replied with a smile.

"Did your grandfather ever talk about any confrontations he might have gotten into?" I asked.

She thought for a brief moment, then shook her head.

"He didn't mention anything about running off drug dealers from the school grounds?"

Her eyes widened. "No. Did he do that?"

"It seems so," I said.

Haley put two and two together quickly. "And you think they may have retaliated against him?"

I nodded. "Could be?" I took a deep breath. "It's all we have to go on right now."

"How long are you in town for?" JD asked.

"Until I get everything sorted," Haley said. "I've got a really flexible job, so I can work from anywhere."

"What do you do?"

She hesitated for a long moment. "I'd rather not say."

That got JD's attention. He arched a curious eyebrow. "Now I'm intrigued."

"A woman should always have a little mystery about her," she said with a coy smile.

"You know he's thinking something dirty," I said.

Haley shrugged. "I can't control what goes on in his mind."

"I don't think *he* can control what goes on in his mind," I said.

Haley laughed.

"Is it dirty?" JD asked, not able to help himself.

She smacked his arm playfully. "No. Cleaning out sewer lines is dirty. What I do is clean," she said with the sly smile.

We laughed.

Haley wasn't divulging any information. I think she enjoyed making us wonder.

The waitress, Isla, sauntered by, and we ordered another round of beer. She returned a few moments later with three ice cold long necks. JD's eyes were glued to her assets as she strutted away.

"To Warren," Haley said, lifting her beer.

"To Warren," we replied, clinking bottles.

"Uh, oh!" Jack muttered. "Here comes trouble."

I followed his eyes toward the door. Jordyn entered, clinging on to some guy's arm.

I was kinda hoping she didn't notice us, but there was no chance of that. Her eyes lit up, and she ran toward us. She gave us both a hug, and her breath reeked of whiskey. "Oh my God. I'm so glad I ran into you both."

She was already slurring her words.

"I made such an ass out of myself the other day. I hope you guys can forgive me? I'm not always that sloppy of a drunk."

The dude she was with hovered around the table.

"Oh, Jack, Tyson, this is my boyfriend, Bryce."

We shook.

"You're Denise's boyfriend? Right?" Bryce asked.

"Yes, he is," Jordyn said before I could answer.

She had clearly made up some story. She sure as hell didn't act like she had a boyfriend the other day.

There was an awkward moment of silence.

Jordyn was hot, and her bikini top was holding on for dear life, but I was glad I didn't have to babysit her tonight. Another few drinks, and she'd be in the obnoxious zone—if she wasn't there already.

"Well, it was good to see you both!" Jordyn smiled and drifted away with her *boyfriend*.

Haley flashed me a curious look.

"Friend of a friend," I explained.

It wasn't 15 minutes later when Jordyn was practically banging Bryce at the bar. They were locked at the lips, and their hips mashed together. The two were going at it hot and heavy when Jordyn lost her balance and fell back into a burly guy next to her, spilling his drink. The glass dropped from his hand and shattered against the concrete floor, spraying shards in all directions.

Jordyn laughed. "Whoops. My bad!"

"No problem," the guy said. "Just buy me another one."

He was calm and cordial.

Jordyn's face crinkled. "Fuck you! I'm not buying you shit."

The man's face soured. "That was a $10 cocktail, and somebody's gonna buy me another one."

"What's the matter?" Jordyn asked. "You can't afford $10?"

"You seem like the one who can't afford $10. How about we take it out in trade?" The burly man flashed a lecherous smile. "You can put that pretty little mouth to work, and we'll call it even."

That's when Bryce puffed up. "Hey man. Take it easy."

"Or what?" The burly man scowled at him.

Bryce tensed. "Look, I'll buy you another drink."

"What if I'd rather have your girlfriend blow me?"

Bryce grew red in the face, and the veins in his neck bulged. His hands balled into fists.

I could tell this was gonna end badly. The barrel-chested man had gone to the dark side. He was ready to rumble.

I launched from the table and dashed across the bar, flashing my badge as I approached. "Deputy Sheriff! Everybody just calm down. I'm sure the lady would be more than happy to buy you another drink, won't you?"

My eyes blazed into Jordyn.

Jordyn sighed. "Fine. I'll buy the fat fuck a drink."

The burly man clenched his jaw.

"Bro, have another one on the house," the bartender said.

He'd been watching the whole thing and was trying to avert disaster. He mixed another cocktail and slid it across the bar to the big man.

The thick tension seemed to settle.

"Is everybody cool now?" I asked.

The burly man was silent for a long moment. "Yeah. We're cool." He paused for a moment. It was the calm before the storm. "I still want her to suck my—"

He didn't even get to finish his thought. Bryce swung a hard right. His fist careened through the air, over Jordyn's head, connecting with the burly man's cheek.

I grumbled to myself knowing I was about to get in the middle of it.

21

Bryce's knuckles connected with the burly man's cheek. The smack echoed throughout the bar. Bryce had swung with all his might. Still, it barely budged the big guy.

Bryce's eyes widened, realizing what he had gotten himself into.

The burly man squared his jaw, reared his fist back, and clocked Bryce. The punch knocked him out cold. He fell to the concrete like a rock—nothing to break his fall except his face.

Jordyn shrieked in terror.

"Easy there, big guy," I said.

He glared at me, his eyes still filled with rage. In the blink of an eye, his fist careened toward me.

Shit!

I ducked and side-stepped.

His massive fist whooshed overhead.

I backed away as we squared off against each other again. "I don't think you want to do this. Assaulting an officer has serious—"

He charged and swung hard.

I sidestepped again, blocked and grabbed his forearm, punched him in the rib cage, then twisted his arm around behind his back. I took him to the ground in an arm-bar takedown and planted my foot against his spine as I wrenched his arm in a painful direction, bending his wrist. Soft tissue popped and crackled. Another fraction of an inch and something would dislocate.

He groaned in agony.

By that time JD had arrived. He still had his drink in his hand. "Looks like you've got everything under control."

Jack called the Sheriff's Office, and they sent two patrol cars to take Bryce and the burly man away.

I couldn't arrest Jordyn for being an idiot, but I wanted to.

"Did you have to arrest my boyfriend?" she complained.

"He threw the first punch," I said. "That's assault. Maybe you should think before you go mouthing off when you're drunk?"

"You're an asshole," she slurred.

Denise must have gotten wind of the situation, because she showed up in time to take her friend home before Jordyn did something else stupid.

"I don't know what you see in this guy," Jordyn said to Denise. "He's a total loser."

"Come on," Denise said. "I think it's time we get you home."

"I don't want to go home!"

"It's either home, or the county jail."

"Seriously?" Jordyn said. "So, now you're turning on me?"

"Nobody's turning on you, JJ. You've just had a little too much to drink, and things have gotten out of hand."

Denise told me she'd call me later. The sloppy blonde bitched and cursed at me as Denise escorted her out of the bar.

The bar returned to normal, and JD and I returned to our table.

"Never a dull moment in Coconut Key," Haley muttered.

"Did you grow up here?" I asked.

Haley nodded. "Pappy raised me. My father left when I was young. My mother had a substance abuse problem and OD'd. I think I was eight when I went to live with him."

"That's a lot to go through as a kid," I said.

"You gotta take what life gives you." Haley shrugged.

There was a moment of silence.

"Well, I better get home," she said. "I enjoyed it, boys. Thanks for the distraction."

Haley motioned to the waitress for the check.

Jack tried to take the leather folio when it arrived, but Haley insisted. "It's the least I can do. You're risking your life to find Pappy's killer. A few beers is a small price to pay."

Haley stuck a wad of cash in the folio and gave us both a hug before she left.

"She's a sweetheart," Jack said. "I hate to see bad shit happen to good people."

"Well, let's do what we can to make this right."

Jack and I finished our beer, then he drove me back to the marina.

In the morning, Daniels called with another situation. "I need you to get over to the *Seven Seas* and investigate this Peeping Tom thing."

"Does this have anything to do with Warren Russell?" I said, yawning.

"No. But I need somebody who's tech savvy, and right now you fit the bill."

I hung up the phone and pulled myself out of bed. The morning sun blasted the suite. I called JD and told him I'd meet him at the hotel in 15 minutes. I pulled on some clothes, grabbed my helmet and gloves, and strolled down the dock to my sport bike. The two-wheeled demon was just one step short of a Moto XP racing bike. It was like straddling a rocket. Twisting the throttle would launch you into another dimension. I cranked up the X6 and revved the engine. The musical exhaust note echoed through the cool morning air. I let out the clutch and raced across town.

Jack's lime-green Porsche was in the hotel parking lot when

I arrived. I parked next to him, peeled off my helmet, and strolled into the lobby. JD was already having a discussion with the manager, and an irate woman who'd been victimized. Her husband stood beside her, letting her do all the work.

She was blonde, in her mid-30s, and had a rock on her finger the size of a small asteroid. "This is absolutely outrageous. I'm going to sue this hotel into bankruptcy!"

"She found this attached to the smoke detector above the bed," JD said, handing me a small black wireless camera that made a dime look large.

I examined the device.

"I want to know who has that footage," the blonde demanded. "And I want it destroyed, immediately." She had a horrific thought. "Oh, my God! What if that footage is already on the Internet?"

"Mrs. Hebert, we will do everything in our power to discover the source of the problem and minimize the damages," the manager said.

"The damage has been done. My husband and I were in the middle of an intimate act. This is highly illegal. My privacy has been violated!"

"Yes ma'am, and we apologize for any inconvenience this may have caused."

"Inconvenience?" Mrs. Hebert looked like her head was about to explode. She growled at the man.

"This is a consumer grade camera," I said. "The range can't be very far. Where is your IT guy? It's likely this device was connected to your network. If there's one device, there could be others."

The manager went pale. "Others?"

"I need a list of everyone who had access to that room," I said. "The housecleaning staff, maintenance, front desk workers, security personnel..."

The manager thought about it for a moment. "We don't know if that camera was planted by a hotel employee. That could have been placed by a previous guest."

It was clear he was trying to create some wiggle room to avoid liability.

He picked up the phone, dialed an extension, and said, "I need you to get to the front desk. Now!"

A few moments later, the IT guy strolled to the desk. Sean was a skinny guy, with shaggy hair, glasses, and looked in his early 20s. The manager explained the situation to him.

He shrugged. "What do you want me to do about it?"

"I want you to figure out if these devices are connected to our network, and who may have done this?"

"Well, it wasn't me, if that's what you're thinking."

"You have the know-how and the access," I said.

"I can show you the network, and every device connected to it." Sean said.

JD stayed with Mrs. Hebert, and I followed Sean to the server room. It was a climate controlled area with a tall tower that managed the hotel's network and access points. Cooling fans within the server hummed.

"Who has access to this room?" I asked.

"Me. The manager. Security personnel." He closed and locked the door, then led me to his office. It was just down the hall. "This is where I work. I have access to the network, and I can manage all the wireless access points."

Sean sat behind the desk and pulled up a network monitoring app. He clicked a few tabs then scrolled through a list. "This is every device connected to the network. We have several different access points throughout the hotel. Here you can see each device connected to the individual access points. There was a long list of personal computers, cell phones, tablets—each had a unique name and ID number. The list was constantly changing as new devices logged on and off the network.

"Each guest needs a unique password to access the device. Usually the room number plus their last name." He scrolled through the long list. "It's going to be tough to identify a specific device. There are so many, and some of them are just listed by an ID number."

Sean kept scanning the list. "Hang on. *SHDcam-2279-a. SHDcam-3126-j. SHDcam-8139-x*. Those look like cameras to me."

Sean found a dozen more listed like that in the connected devices.

"Is there any way to tell which rooms these are in?" I asked.

"Manual inspection."

"How would someone go about connecting these devices to the network?"

"The setup process on most of these devices is fairly simple. They would just log onto the network, enter the passcode, and connect the device. Whoever was using these cameras probably did so through an app on a cell phone or tablet."

"How would they get the network passcode?"

"Well, a guest probably couldn't do it. Their passcode only allows them access to web browsing and email. The main server's passcode is on a sticker on the server. Makes it easier in case people forget."

"So anybody with access to that server room could have done this?"

"Sure."

"Do you have any idea who that might be?"

He raised his hands innocently. "Like I said, it wasn't me."

"Are there any other IT personnel?" I asked. "Who covers the night shift?"

22

It was an *IT emergency*.

Too much for Sean to handle.

That's what I told the manager to tell Zeke—the night shift nerd in charge of the hotel's computer network. The request would appeal to his ego. The ruse was a lot easier than going to him. Zeke was one of the few people that had access to the server room and knew the master passcode to the network.

We hung out in the lobby of the Seven Seas, waiting for Zeke to arrive.

Tony Scarpetti strolled through the doors, and a grin curled on his face when he saw us. "Well, if it isn't my two favorite cops."

We shook hands.

Big Tony was a former gangster who had turned legit. He ran an ongoing, high-stakes poker game in a suite at the *Seven Seas*. It was a classy operation, and I had pulled my fair share of winnings from the regular event. Jack and I had helped Tony out of a tight spot a while back, and we had become friends—in an odd sort of way. Tony was adamant that he was now a legitimate businessman, but I knew he still had deep Mafia connections.

"What gives?" Tony said. "You get rich and famous and you stop coming around my game?"

I shrugged, apologetically. "It's been kind of crazy lately. I swear, I'll stop by soon and you can deal me in."

"You two need anything, let me know. I mean it. Anything."

Tony didn't make that kind of offer lightly. He was a good guy to have on your side. He could also be a nightmare of an enemy. His Mafia connections were just a phone call away.

"Thanks, Tony," I said.

We shook hands again, and he patted me on the shoulder before strolling toward the bar.

Zeke staggered into the lobby 30 minutes later, looking sleep deprived. He was 6" tall, brown matted hair, round belly, and a thin mustache that looked like something a high school kid would grow, even though Zeke was in his early 30s.

"What's the major malfunction that Sean couldn't handle?" Zeke said as he strutted into the lobby.

I flashed my badge. "Deputy Sheriff. We'd like to talk to you for a minute."

"Sure, no problem," he said, maintaining his cool. Then he spun around and darted into the parking lot.

I chased after him.

It wasn't going to be much of a chase.

When I caught up to him, I slammed his face into the hood of a car and ratcheted a pair of cuffs around his wrists. The sheet metal reverberated, and Zeke groaned from the impact.

"What's going on?"

"You're under arrest for illegal videography."

"What are you talking about?" he asked, as I yanked him from the car and marched him toward the lobby.

"Really? You're going to play dumb?" I asked.

"I'm smart enough to know better than to talk to you."

"How many cameras have you placed throughout the hotel?"

"What part of *I'm not talking to you* do you not understand?"

"You do realize the penalties for recording someone in an area where they have an expectation of privacy?"

Zeke said nothing.

"I'd start cooperating if I were you," I said. "You don't look like the kind of guy who would do well in jail. A guy like you is gonna be on his knees most of the time."

The color drained from Zeke's face, and sweat misted on his skin.

Jack called Sheriff Daniels, and within moments, a patrol car arrived and escorted Zeke to the County Jail.

I was pretty sure that Zeke was responsible for the whole

thing, but I couldn't rule out the possibility that he acted with an accomplice. Perhaps Sean? I needed to get the computer forensics team down here and analyze the server and make a backup copy of the drives if necessary. Perhaps even confiscate the device?

"You want to do what?" the manager exclaimed when I told him of my plan.

"We don't know if there is any footage stored on the server," I said. "We need to be able to analyze the hard drives and determine exactly how many cameras were placed, when, and if possible, by whom."

"We know *who*," the manager said.

"The more evidence I have, the more solid a case we can make. You wouldn't want to be seen as uncooperative, would you?"

"That server houses our entire reservation system. All the Wi-Fi, and entertainment services to the rooms."

I shrugged, then snidely added. "Maybe you should vet your employees a little better?"

The manager frowned, nervously. "I'll need to call my superior."

"Do what you need to do. But nobody touches that server until our forensics team has taken a look. In the meantime, we need to do a sweep of every room on the premises, looking for surveillance devices."

Sweat sprouted from his forehead. "If word of this gets out, this hotel could be ruined."

"I'm willing to keep my mouth shut, for a price," Mrs. Hebert said with an arched eyebrow.

The manager swallowed hard. "I'm sure we can come to some kind of arrangement. I will have to speak with my superior."

The manager made his phone call.

We didn't specifically have a computer crimes unit, but Daniels sent our own nerd herd from the information systems department. They were responsible for running the network for the Sheriff's Department and knew their way around this type of thing better than I did.

Matthew and Aiden took a look at the server. Matthew was shorter with brown hair and brown eyes, Aiden was tall and skinny with shaggy blonde hair. Both were in their early 20s. After taking a cursory glance at the system, Aiden said, "The easiest thing to do would be to clone the drive, then we can sift through the data at our leisure. That would minimize disruption of hotel operations."

"Whatever minimizes disruption of operations, I'm in favor of," the manager said. Then he added, "Do you need a warrant for this?"

I glared at him. "Do you want to make us jump through hoops? Or do you want this resolved before the media gets hold of it?"

"Quick and quiet," the manager said.

"They've only got 10 TB of data storage." Aiden said. "We can clone that pretty easily."

"I'll leave the task in your capable hands," I said. "Let me know what you find."

Aiden gave me a mock salute.

I left the two computer gurus in the server room and strolled back to the lobby with the hotel manager.

JD had begun searching the hotel rooms for additional surveillance devices with the hotel security staff. I caught up with him, and after several hours of searching for devices, we found cameras positioned in bed rooms and bathrooms of multiple units.

The hotel manager looked like he was going to be sick. "This is going to ruin us. There's no telling how many people were videotaped, doing God knows what."

"I hope you have a good public relations firm," JD said.

"I need to call my supervisor again," the manager said.

He hustled out of the room.

Once we had searched all the rooms, we headed back to the Sheriff's Office and logged the cameras as evidence. I was sure the crime lab would be able to pull a fingerprint from one of the devices. We had a good case against Zeke.

JD and I filled out paperwork in the conference room. With that incident wrapped up, it was time to get back to work on Warren's case. The middle school would be letting out soon, and I wanted to take another gander around campus.

23

A line of yellow buses roared out of the parking lot. The parent pick up lane was jam-packed. Kids walked through the crosswalk, lugging backpacks, carrying books, listening to headphones. Marcy wore her lime-green vest, ushering students from one side of the street to the other.

Most kids didn't use the crosswalk.

I had Lana's sketch of the suspect on my iPhone. I studied it again as I scanned the crowd. We rolled through the school zone in Jack's Porsche. I had left my bike at the station. We probably looked like a couple of predators, circling the school several times.

I told JD to turn down one of the side streets and cruise through the neighborhoods near the school. If I were a drug dealer, I wouldn't be slinging dope right in front of the school... I would try to be a little less conspicuous.

Sure enough, we saw the boy with the baggy pants and eagle backpack. I looked at the suspect sketch, then the boy. The resemblance was spot on. He was talking to another kid. Money exchanged hands, as well as a small balloon less than the size of a marble. The slick transfer took place during a handshake.

Bingo!

Jack rolled up to the transaction in the lizard-green sports car. We didn't look like your average cops—not in a car like this. What cop, who's not on the take, can afford a $275,000 exotic?

"Hey, can you hook me up?" I said to the kid in the baggy pants.

His suspicious eyes flicked from me to JD. Then he spun around and took off running.

I grumbled under my breath as I launched out of the car. I sprinted down the sidewalk, chasing after the kid. He couldn't have been more than 17. And he was fast!

Real fast.

My chest heaved for breath, and my legs drove me forward.

He veered left and darted up a driveway, then plowed through the gate.

I followed in time to see him run across the backyard and scale the fence.

This wasn't his first rodeo.

He'd run from the cops before, and he knew the drill.

But the backpack slowed him down a little. I figured it was mostly for show. There were probably a few books in it in case someone stopped him and asked him questions. But the street dealers had gotten pretty savvy. They typically carried drugs in small balloons that they kept in their mouths. They could swallow them in case of trouble and wait till the merchandise came out on the other side.

The street dealers never kept anything in their pockets.

I wasn't beyond letting him sit in a cell until the evidence materialized—*providing I could catch up with him.*

I hurtled the fence and landed in another yard with two yappy dogs that went batshit crazy when they saw the two of us.

In a flash, the punk was up and over another fence.

I vaulted over the fence behind him, and when I hit the ground, the blade of a shovel careened toward my face.

A yard crew was putting in drainage pipes—4" thick, schedule 40 PVC that ran down to the front curb. The crew must have been on break, and the punk grabbed one of their shovels. He swung as hard as he could.

I ducked below the shovel as it swished overhead.

He backhanded the blade toward me again.

I grabbed the shaft, then lunged the shovel forward, punching the handle into his gut. All the balloons he was holding in his mouth spewed onto the yard as he coughed.

I pounced on him, grabbed his wrists, and slapped the cuffs on him as fast as I could. "Looks like today's your lucky day."

"Fuck you!"

His right hand had cuts and bruises on it, like he'd recently been in a fight.

A one sided fight.

"Those are some pretty nasty cuts on your knuckles. Whose ass did you kick?"

"Fuck you! Get off me!"

"Oh, by the way. You're under arrest."

"You ain't no cop."

"Then why did you run?"

"My mom told me never talk to strangers."

I yanked him to his feet and walked him out to the street. Once I knew where I was, I called the Sheriff's Office and had them send a patrol car to pick up the perp. When they arrived, I handed the little miscreant off, then went back to the yard and collected the balloons he'd spit out of his mouth. I didn't know what was in them. Cocaine, crack, methamphetamine, maybe even heroin?

24

"I told you, I ain't sayin' shit," the punk said. "I don't talk to the police."

The kids sat at a table in an interrogation room.

"What's your name, kid?" I asked.

"I don't gotta tell you."

"Makes no difference to me. You're going to sit here just the same."

He stared me down, trying to act tough.

"Since you don't have a name, how about I call you *dumbass*?"

He snarled at me. "How about I call you *bitch, I'll whoop your ass!*"

I laughed. "Where you're going, you will most certainly be somebody's bitch."

He clammed up after that.

"Want to tell me how you got those cuts on your hand?"

"Eating pussy," he quipped.

"I think you're doing it wrong, kid."

He continued to stare at me, keeping up the tough guy act.

"You're looking at a long stretch," I said.

"Man, you can't touch me. I'm 17. I'm a juvenile. They're gonna slap me on the wrist, and I'm gonna walk away."

I laughed. "You think this is just about the drugs, don't you?"

His face crinkled at me. Then he asked innocently, "Drugs? What drugs?"

"I'm sure that wasn't baking soda in those balloons."

"I don't know what you're talking about. You planted that shit." He paused. "Matter of fact, I remember you grabbing my junk after you put the handcuffs on me. Then you said you'd let me go if I blew you. That's what I remember." A smug grin curled on his face.

I glared at him. This kid thought he could beat the system. Up to this point, he didn't have a criminal record. It seemed like he'd been beating the system for a long time. This wasn't the first day that he'd been dealing drugs on a street corner.

"Making a false complaint is a criminal offense," I said.

"What about making a false arrest? The way I see it, a predator like you ought to be in jail."

I wanted to smack the cocky grin from his face.

JD pulled open the door and motioned for me to exit. There was a sparkle in his eyes. I knew he had something interesting to say.

I stepped into the hallway and closed the door to the interrogation room behind me.

"This little shithead's fingerprints match those on the drawer handles in Warren's bedroom. That puts him at the scene of the crime."

"Do we know his name yet?" I asked.

"Denise sent the sketch to the principal at the high school. He said it looked like Davon Jones. I pulled up his social media profile." Jack showed me the display on his phone.

Sure enough, we had put a name to our suspect.

A slight grin tugged on my lips. I spun around and pushed back into the interrogation room. "Davon Jones… " I said as I walked into the room, letting it hang in the air for moment

His eyes went wide. "Aw, man!"

"You think I wouldn't figure it out?"

"Big deal. So you know my name? That doesn't change the fact that you're a creepy motherfucker that likes little boys."

"Do you know Warren Russell?" I asked.

"Who?" he asked with a scowl.

"So, you'd have no reason to be in his home?"

"Hell no! I don't even know who you're talking about."

"The dead old man. I'm sure you'd recognize him if you saw

him. He was beaten to death by a right-hander. We found your fingerprints inside his home. Care to explain that?"

The punk's smug grin faded.

"You could have probably pleaded down the drug charge. Not served any time. First offense. You could have probably walked with probation. But murder? You're gonna be a really old man before you see daylight again. Because guess what... in this state, you can be tried as an adult."

Davon swallowed hard. "Bullshit."

"Hand to God. In a capital case like this, you'll be tried with the big boys. No slap on the wrist. No clean record when you turn 18."

Sweat misted on Davon's skin.

"At this point, it's open and shut. I've got your prints. I've got a witness who saw you enter the house. You're toast."

I didn't have a witness, but Davon didn't know that.

His hands trembled slightly. "Look, man. I didn't have nothing to do with that old man dying. He was already dead when I got to the house."

"Really?"

"I swear to God. He was dead on the living room floor. Somebody put a hurting on him real bad."

"I don't suppose you know who this *somebody* is?"

"I'd tell you if I knew. But I don't know shit."

"What time were you there?"

Davon shrugged. "Midnight."

"What were you doing?"

Davon was silent a moment.

"Go ahead. Keep quiet. Makes no difference to me. Like I said, I got enough to put you away for this, whether you did it or not."

Davon grumbled to himself. "The old man was always getting up in my shit. See, I'm a businessman. I'm just trying to do business. He was interfering with my place of employment. I mean, if people didn't want my product, I'd be out of business. I ain't the problem. Don't hate the player, hate the game."

"So you decided to go to the house and rough him up?"

"Man, pull your head out of your ass. I didn't decide shit. I don't decide nothing. I do what I'm told."

"Who told you?"

"Shit, I tell you that, then I'll really be dead."

25

"He can proclaim his innocence until the cows come home, but that doesn't necessarily make it so," JD said.

We stood in the hallway with Sheriff Daniels outside the interrogation room.

"We've got more than enough to make a case," Daniels said. "I'm pretty confident the DA will want to move forward. A kid like this is just a mule for a bigger dealer. And I guarantee you, his replacement is already on the street. Formal charges may put enough pressure on him to reveal his employer. We might be able to get the big boss on a conspiracy charge, if nothing else. Let's see how this little punk reacts after a few days in a cell, staring down the barrel of a life term. I'm guessing he'll start to sing real quick."

"With the abrasions on his hand, there could be trace DNA on Warren's cheek," I said. "Has Brenda found any?"

"I think she's still waiting on the lab results," Daniels said.

"In the meantime, see if you can figure out who this kid is hustling for."

"You got it, boss," JD said.

"How's your dad doing?" I asked.

Daniels sighed. "Holding steady, I guess. I'm looking around at the facilities here. It all kind of seems like a nightmare. I don't want to put him into a place where he'll be ignored. I hear horror stories of elderly laying in pools of piss and shit for hours while waiting on someone to take them to the bathroom."

JD and I cringed at the thought.

"You've been to C-KALF?" Daniels asked. "What did you think of the place?"

I shrugged. "It seemed clean. The staff was attentive, I guess."

"The reviews online seem okay. None of these places get great ratings, to tell you the truth." Daniels paused.

"I'll see what I can find out," I said.

"Well, I've got to do something quick," Daniels said. "I worry about Dad living alone."

"Let us know if there's anything we can do," I said.

We left the Sheriff's Office, and JD followed me back to the marina. I took Buddy for a walk. Afterward, we headed to *Wetsuit* for happy hour. Jack couldn't get enough of the waitresses in skintight neoprene. They looked like they belonged in a Bond movie.

"You two are getting to be regulars," Isla said as she took our order.

She had straight brunette hair, blue eyes, long lashes, and a body worthy of her Brazilian heritage.

"Two whiskeys on the rocks," Jack said.

"Coming right up!" Isla sauntered away, and her assets drew our lingering stares.

You could tell the girl spent a lot of time in the gym doing bridges, lunges, and Belgian split squats.

It was early still, and the Friday night crowd hadn't flooded in yet. Attendance was still pretty thin, and the music was at a reasonable volume.

Isla returned a moment later with our drinks. The bombshell flashed a brilliant smile as she set my beverage in front of me. Her eyes sparkled. "I'll be back to check on you boys shortly. If you need anything, *anything* at all, just holler."

With that, she sauntered away. Once again, Jack and I both couldn't resist the urge to follow her with our eyes.

"I believe she could make a dead man walk." Jack lifted his glass.

We toasted, clinking glasses.

Jack took a sip and gasped. "God, I love this town."

Despite all the chaos, Coconut Key certainly had its merits. It was like being on a perpetual vacation.

"Oh shit," I muttered as I looked across the bar.

"What is it?"

I hung my head low, obscuring my face. I didn't want to be seen. I muttered, "Jordyn."

Jack just *had* to crane his neck over his shoulder and look.

Jordyn saw him. She made a beeline straight toward us.

I lifted my head. It was no use hiding now.

"Hey! What's up, boys?" Jordyn said with a sparkling smile, like nothing had ever happened.

"Not much," I said.

She made a sad face and spoke in a baby doll voice. "Are you still mad at me for the other night?"

I looked at her flatly. "You did cause quite a commotion."

She shrugged. "Shit happens."

I rolled my eyes. "Maybe you should ease up on the drinking?"

"Where's the fun in that?" She paused, then conceded, "Okay, maybe I can be a little excessive at times, but I'd rather live life on the edge than in the middle."

"Where's your boyfriend?" I asked.

"Why? You interested?" A seductive glimmer flickered in her eyes.

"I am," Jack said.

She laughed. "He's not my boyfriend."

"He sure looked like it the other night?" I said.

"Whatever. I told him I wanted to see other people. It's not my fault if he still thinks I'm his girlfriend. I told him I'm not." She sighed. "Some people are in denial."

"Well, hopefully you can stay out of trouble tonight," I said.

A sly grin curled on her full lips. "Honey, I'm always looking for trouble." She paused. "I'm out with my girlfriends. Come join us?"

She motioned to a table across the bar with two hotties.

"Maybe some other time," I said.

She frowned and turned out her bottom lip. "I'm starting to get the feeling you don't like me."

"Whatever gave you that idea?" I said, dryly.

She inhaled deeply, then sighed dramatically. "If you don't want to hang out with three gorgeous girls, I guess it's your loss."

She lingered for a moment, then spun around and headed back to her friends, putting a little extra sway into her hips.

Jack looked at me like I was crazy. "What the hell is wrong with you?"

My face crinkled. "That girl is batshit crazy."

"Yeah, but her friends might not be. Besides... *psychosex*. You know that girl will do all kinds of freaky shit."

"You were the one who suggested I stay away from her."

"I never said that."

"Yes you did!"

"I said that I would pick Denise over her." He pretended to

look around. "But I don't see Denise. And you just turned down your only option."

"She's not my only option. The waitress seemed nice."

"Isla only smiled at you because she wants a big tip," JD said.

I sneered at him. "How many waitresses have you dated?"

He shrugged. "A lot."

"I rest my case."

"It's fine if you want to remain celibate. But don't screw things up for me," Jack said.

I laughed. "If you want to go over there and immerse yourself in the drama, be my guest."

"We don't know if her friends are as batshit crazy as she is."

"I admire your optimism," I said. "Why don't you go find out and report back."

My challenge was accepted. Jack pushed back from the table. "I will return shortly... or not."

He strutted across the bar to the table of lovely ladies.

I just shook my head.

Within a few seconds of approaching the table, Jack had them laughing. He had his charm, that was for sure. I could only imagine the stories I would hear in the morning.

My phone buzzed in my pocket, and I took the call. Scarlett's squeaky voice blasted through the speaker. "Tyson, I need your help!" She said in a sob. "I think I screwed up."

26

"Slow down, take a deep breath. What's going on?" I asked.

Scarlet continued to sob. "He attacked me!"

My blood boiled. My veins bulged. "Who?"

"My acting coach. Easton."

"Are you okay?"

"Yeah, but my career is fucked!"

"Tell me exactly what happened."

She sniffled and blew her nose. Scarlett took a deep breath, then continued. "I went to a couple classes, and he seemed like a really nice guy. He told me I had talent and a lot of potential. He really seemed enthusiastic about my career. He wanted to put me on the fast track and offered private coaching."

I knew exactly where the story was going.

"So, we were at the studio, alone, after class one night. That's when he made the moves on me. I told him I wasn't interested, and that I didn't want to make a career that way. He pinned me to the ground, got on top of me..."

At this point I was about to explode.

Scarlett continued. "I kneed him in the balls, slithered from underneath him, and ran out of the studio. Then I caught a cab back to the apartment." She hesitated. "My career is over. Do you understand how influential the guy is?"

"Fuck that guy," I said. "You don't need him. You don't need anybody."

"Yeah," she muttered, dejected.

"I'm serious. That guy doesn't have as much power as you think he does."

"He can badmouth me to everybody that matters in this town."

"Not if I have anything to say about it," I said.

"Don't tell Jack," Scarlett said. "I don't want him getting upset. He'll tell me to come back to Coconut Key. I just can't deal with getting into a fight with him right now."

I glanced across the bar to Jack. She was making a big *ask*.

"I don't know what to do," Scarlett cried. "Can you come out here?"

"I'm on the next plane. I'll talk to Joel, and we'll get this sorted out. Have you made a police report?"

"No! I'm not doing that. That's career suicide. Nobody, and I mean nobody, will work with me if I start making those kinds of allegations."

"Just sit tight. And don't go back to his class."

"You don't have to worry about that."

I hung up the phone and called Joel. "We have a situation."

"Is this about Easton?" Joel asked. He already knew.

"What did he say to you?"

"He called, said he wouldn't be able to work with Scarlett anymore. Said she had a bad attitude. Said she came on to him and offered to exchange sexual favors if he would advance her career."

"That son-of-a-bitch!"

"I gotta be honest with you, this isn't good." Joel paused.

"He attacked her!"

Joel sighed. "Easton can be a little… aggressive."

"So, this isn't the first time this has happened?"

"Easton has helped launch the career of many aspiring actresses over the years. There are a lot of people in this town that are perfectly fine with a little *quid pro quo* to advance their career."

"You're not condoning his activity, are you?" I said, incensed.

"No. Absolutely not. What I'm saying… is that Scarlett needs to pick her battles carefully. If she wants to go *scorched earth*, that's fine. There may be repercussions. That's all I'm saying."

My anger boiled.

"You understand, this puts me in an awkward position. You're my client. I like you. We've made good money together. I think we have the potential to make a lot more. I took Scarlett on because you asked me to. I like her, and I think she has potential in this industry. I wouldn't rep her if I didn't think she had what it takes. But I know that she's on probation, and she's had issues in her past. If what she says happened, I believe it, but if I go to bat for her, it could have ramifications against me and the agency. I know that sounds messed up. But right now, it's *he said, she said*."

"In the current climate, it could have negative ramifications for your agency if you dismiss her claims."

"I am aware of that as well." Joel sighed. "It's up to you. Right now you are *up-and-coming*. You've got a little heat with this recent sale, and the studio wanting to produce a television show. If the Bree Taylor story is a hit, you can write your own ticket. I'm not sure I would jeopardize that right now."

"You're not really suggesting I keep my mouth shut to save my career, are you? I don't care about any of that."

"I like a man with integrity. It's rare around here."

"I'm heading out on the next flight. We can talk more when I get to Los Angeles."

"Take the flight, talk to Scarlett, see how you two want to handle this. I'll stand behind you both whatever you decide."

"Thanks, Joel. I appreciate that. This guy can't continue to behave that way."

"For your own sake, just make sure she is telling it exactly as it happened."

27

This time I didn't have a private plane at my disposal. I looked at flights online, and it was a nightmare. The last flight left Coconut Key at 9:30 PM. There was a stop in Chicago, and the flight would arrive in Los Angeles at 11:30 AM.

Not my first choice.

There was barely enough time to make it back to the *Vivere*, pack a bag, and get to the airport. I made some excuse to Jack about an emergency production meeting with the studio. He didn't really pay attention. He was more than happy to stay at *Wetsuit* and ply his craft.

I caught a cab back to the marina, gathered my things, and left Buddy and Fluffy with Madison. I felt bad keeping the situation from JD, but after his recent heart episode, I figured he didn't need the added stress.

I bought a first class ticket. The flight wasn't full, and I was able to snag a deal online. I boarded the plane, took my seat, and we were wheels up by 9:35 PM. With any luck, I'd be in Los Angeles by noon.

A pretty blonde named Kennedy took my drink order. She told me I had a meal choice of either chicken parmesan, or lasagna.

I picked the lasagna.

"You look familiar," she said. "Have we met before?"

I studied her gorgeous face. "I'm pretty sure I'd remember a woman like you."

She blushed and batted her eyelashes.

"I know we've met. Give me a minute. I'll think of it," she said as she headed to the galley.

There were two other people in first class, and not many in coach. I reclined my seat back and sunk into the soft leather. Flying private jets across the country had spoiled me. As nice as the accommodations were, it seemed cramped and uncomfortable in comparison. The FBO terminal was so much easier to navigate. And security at the FBO was a breeze. For this flight, I had checked my roller case and had complied with all the TSA regulations for traveling with a firearm.

Kennedy returned shortly with a glass of whiskey on the rocks. She set it on the fold-out tray atop a napkin. She flashed another brilliant smile. "Please let me know if there's anything else I can do for you."

She spun around and strutted back to the galley. She certainly made the uniform look good. With a short blonde bob, blue eyes, and sculpted cheekbones, she made flying commercial almost bearable.

The fasten seatbelt sign went out, and the pilot crackled over the intercom. "Folks, it looks like we'll have pretty smooth air. I turned off the fasten seatbelt sign. You are free to move about the cabin, but please keep your seatbelt fastened while seated." He had the typical pilot's voice that was smooth and fast like a radio DJ. "Estimated flight time to Chicago is 4 hours, 20 minutes. Sit back, relax, and enjoy the flight."

I yawned and swallowed, trying to get my ears to pop.

Kennedy returned a few moments later with a sly grin on her face. "You were the guy who broke up the fight at *Wetsuit*."

"You were there?"

"I had a layover in Coconut Key. You were with that guy that looked like the lead singer of... I can't think of his name..."

"Jack."

"No. Vince? Maybe?"

"Jack's my friend's name."

"Ah. Small world," she said.

"Yes it is."

Kennedy went about her business, serving the other flyers, but she kept stopping by to chat throughout the flight.

"Are you based in Chicago?" I asked.

"Yes, but I'm originally from Texas."

"How do you like Chicago?"

"I like it. It's a great city. A little too cold sometimes. I'm still getting used to it. I was based out of Houston, which is also a hub for the airline, so it was a pretty easy move. We have two seasons in Houston. Hot and hotter. So, Chicago is definitely a change of pace."

I chuckled. I knew how hot Texas summers could be.

"So, you're a deputy?"

I raised my brow. "You're observant."

"I'm telling you. I watched that whole thing go down. It was great entertainment. The chick that started it was a nut job." Kennedy cringed. "I must say, I was a little worried for you. That was a big guy that swung at you."

"I've fought bigger," I said with a grin.

She smiled. "Well, I really should pretend like there are other people on this plane."

We chatted a few more times, and before the flight was over, she slipped her phone number to me on a napkin. She leaned in and whispered into my ear. "I never do this, but since we kind of, sort of, met before the flight, I guess it's okay."

I smiled and texted her so she'd have my number. Thoughts of the mile high club danced in my mind.

It was just before 2 AM when we landed in Chicago. My connecting flight didn't leave till 9:05 AM. I smiled and said goodbye to Kennedy as I de-planed, then strolled up the jetway into the terminal at O'Hare.

Not my favorite airport.

It was such a busy hub, flights were always getting delayed. But right now, it was nearly empty.

I took a seat and tried to get comfortable at the gate.

That was impossible.

There was no way to sprawl out on the seats. The armrests blocked any attempt at reclining. I figured I could roll up a newspaper and sleep on the floor for a few hours until my flight. Or I could spring for a room at the Hilton.

At this time of night, the airport was practically deserted. All the bars and restaurants were closed. The only options were vending machines containing soda, water, and snacks.

I sat there, contemplating my options, watching the rest of the passengers de-plane. The crew followed shortly thereafter, and Kennedy rolled her suitcase out of the jetway. She smiled and waved to me as she walked with a group of flight attendants. Her high heels clacked against the tile as she and her companions strutted away.

I soaked in a last glimpse of her luscious form, then slouched down in the seat, leaned back, and closed my eyes. I'd slept in worse places, but this wasn't going to be any fun. I was about to get up and move to the floor when a sweet voice whispered, "You're not really going to sleep here, are you?"

I peeled my eyes open to see Kennedy hovering over me.

"That was the plan," I said. "But I'm not sure it's a good one."

Kennedy looked at her watch. "The hotel bar is open till 2 AM. It's right across the street. We've got time for a drink. You can decide where you'd rather stay. The terminal? Or, my apartment—if you play your cards right?"

I lifted a curious eyebrow. "I'm pretty good at cards."

"I'm sure you are."

28

The alarm on my phone blasted at 6 AM.

I grabbed the phone and shut off the alarm, then forced myself to sit up. My eyes were glued shut, and I almost had to manually peel them open.

Let's just say I didn't get much sleep the night before.

Kennedy groaned and rolled over in the bed beside me. The sheets twisted as she turned, revealing her naked body. Her glorious backside looked just as enticing as it had the night before.

I crawled out of bed, took a quick shower, and got dressed. I gave Kennedy a light kiss on the cheek before I left. She was asleep and barely acknowledged it.

If I was ever in Chicago, I would definitely fly those skies again.

The line to get through security wasn't too bad since I arrived at the airport so early. The flight was on time, but the service wasn't nearly as good.

It was 11:42 AM when I landed at LAX. I couldn't get a flight into Burbank. I snatched my bag from the carousel at baggage claim and caught a cab at ground transportation. Within moments, I was sitting in traffic on the 405. It was a sea of red taillights.

I suggested an alternate route, taking Sepulveda. The cabdriver just shrugged and said, "It's all the same."

He was probably right.

I texted Scarlett and let her know that I was on the ground.

I had traveled all this way, and I wasn't sure what I was going to do. I knew what I *wanted* to do, but I couldn't just put a bullet in this guy's head.

It took almost an hour to get to the Valley, and when I arrived at the apartment, Scarlett greeted me with a hug. "Are you okay?"

"Yeah, I'm fine," she said in a somber tone. "Thanks for coming. I'm sorry you had to come all the way out here for this."

"Tell me where I find this guy?" I said.

"What are you going to do?"

"Make sure he doesn't do this again."

"You're not going to..."

"No. I'm not going to kill him."

"Because that would probably be bad."

I shrugged. "Probably."

We stood there for a long moment.

"I just want to be perfectly clear in my understanding of what happened," I said.

"What else do you want to know?"

"Did this happen *exactly* as you told me?"

Her face crinkled. "Yes. Why would you even ask that? Do you think I'm lying?"

"Did I say I thought you were lying?"

"Did you even have to ask?"

"I didn't come here to get in a fight with you."

She exhaled. "I'm sorry. I'm just totally stressed out about this."

"Tell me exactly what happened again."

She told me the exact same story as she did before. None of the details had changed. People who make up stories generally can't remember everything they said. Details and time frames tend to change. I knew that Scarlett could sometimes be quite dramatic, but I knew her well enough to know that she was telling the truth, without embellishing.

Rage boiled within.

I left Scarlett's apartment and headed over to the acting studio to give the creep a piece of my mind. It probably wasn't one of my finer moments.

29

"I'm sorry, I'm in the middle of a private lesson," Easton said as I burst in. "If you'd like to audit a class, you can put your name on a waitlist. There should be one at the front desk."

The studio was empty except for Easton and his *protégé*. He sat next to her on the stage. He was dangerously close to her and had his hand on her thigh when I entered the auditorium. There was no one else around. No one at the front desk.

The classroom was a tiny theater with less than 100 seats. The walls were painted black, and a small riser served as a stage. Lights hung from a grid on the ceiling. It was quiet except for the hum of the air-conditioning unit.

I stormed down the aisle, toward the stage, and told the girl, "Private lesson is over. Go home. Find another acting coach!"

A nearby camera on a tripod was aimed at the pair. I made sure it was off.

Easton launched out of his chair. "You can't come in here like this!"

I grabbed the scumbag by the throat and drove him back against the wall. My hand tightened around his trachea, and he clutched my wrist.

"Get out!" I shouted at the girl.

She shrieked and darted out of the theater.

"Do you have any idea who I am?" Easton said, barely able to choke out the words.

"You're a scumbag that forces himself on vulnerable women," I growled.

His face crinkled. "I don't know what you're talking about!"

I tightened my grip on his throat.

"Okay, okay! It won't happen again."

"You're goddamn right it won't! If I hear about this kind of shit again, I don't care if it's even a rumor, I'll be back. And trust me, you don't ever want to see me again." My eyes blazed into him. "Do you understand?"

He nodded.

"Say it!"

"I'll never do it again!"

"And if you try to retaliate against any of these women, because I know there's more than one, you'll regret it. Am I clear?"

He nodded with wide eyes. He could barely breathe, and he

looked like he was about to faint. I pulled my hand away. Easton gasped for breath and collapsed to his knees.

I hovered over him. "Next time you won't get off so easy."

The dirt-ball nodded as he hovered on the ground on all fours.

I wanted to kick him in the face, but I thought better of it. I stormed out of the theater, moved through the empty lobby, and stepped onto the sidewalk in the bright LA sunshine.

A thin smile tugged on my face. Mission accomplished. I took a deep breath and strolled toward the coffee shop on the corner. There was outdoor seating on the sidewalk. I walked past all the people drinking their lattes, wearing sunglasses and yoga pants. I stepped inside, grabbed a coffee with cream and sugar, then caught a cab back to Scarlett's apartment.

"How'd it go?" she asked with worried eyes as I entered.

"I don't think he's going to bother anyone anymore," I said.

"Is he still breathing, or do I want to ask?"

"Relax. I didn't get out of control. I just made a firm suggestion that he change his ways." I smiled.

My phone rang. It was Joel. "What on earth did you do?"

"What do you mean?" I asked, innocently.

"I just got a call from Easton. He said he was accosted in his studio by an angry man who threatened him."

"I don't know what you're talking about," I said.

"This is a big problem. He's livid. He swears that Scarlett will never work in this town. He's going to tell everyone to stay away from her!"

I clenched my jaw. "Apparently he didn't get the message."

"You can't just go barging into people's studio and threaten them," Joel said. "That's not how we do things here."

There was a knock on the door, followed by a gruff voice. "LAPD. We have an arrest warrant."

"You didn't give him my name, did you?" I muttered into the phone.

Joel was silent a moment, then his meek voice filtered through the speaker. "It kind of slipped out."

"I think I'm going to need you to bail me out of jail."

I hung up the phone and pulled open the door to see two LAPD officers with their weapons drawn. "Tyson Wild, we have a warrant for your arrest."

Easton must have been important for the LAPD to respond this fast. Anything under 2 hours was rare.

I raised my hands in the air, turned around, and dropped to my knees. The cold steel cuffs slapped my wrists, then the officers yanked me to my feet.

Scarlett watched with wide eyes. "What's going on?"

"Don't worry," I said. "Everything's gonna be fine."

"You're under arrest for assault with a deadly weapon and making criminal threats. You have the right to remain silent..."

My face twisted at the *deadly weapon* part. I didn't even carry my gun into the studio.

They stuffed me in the back of the patrol car and took me downtown where I was processed, printed, and stuffed into a holding cell with a bunch of lowlifes. The place smelled like body odor and piss. The only thing that ever came out of my mouth was, "I want to speak with an attorney."

I spent the night in that shit-hole, and was arraigned in the morning. Joel contacted my entertainment attorney—the one that had looked over the contract with the studio for the sale of the Bree Taylor story. He was present during the arraignment, and Joel coordinated bail.

By the time I was released, a sea of reporters were waiting. Cameras flashed and news crews shoved microphones in my face. My attorney, Ari Bernstein, said, "Mr. Wild has no comment at this time."

My two representatives ushered me into a limousine, and I slid across the posh leather seats, still wreaking of prison odor. The opulent vehicle was a stark contrast to how I had spent the last 20 hours.

"Easton is saying you pulled a gun on him and threatened to kill him," Ari said.

"I did no such thing!"

"This really isn't my area. I handle contracts. You need to get yourself a good criminal defense attorney. Your next court date is scheduled for the 27th."

I groaned. "You have any recommendations?"

"I can put you in touch with someone," Ari said. "You're

lucky, though. Based on your history, the judge will let you return to Florida as a condition of your bond. That doesn't always happen in felony cases."

The wheels were turning behind Joel's eyes. "This isn't the end of the world. I think I can spin this. It does play into your *bad boy* persona. I've retained a PR firm. BRTW is the best in town. They're not cheap, but they're worth every penny."

"It's his word against my word," I said.

"He's got a witness," Ari added. "One of the students. She corroborates the whole story."

My jaw dropped. "She's lying."

"I don't doubt it," Joel said. "But you picked a fight with a very powerful person. His protégés worship him like he's a cult leader. Nobody in this town will do anything to screw up their career."

I frowned. "Trust me, he has no idea who he just picked a fight with."

Joel's eyes widened. "Okay, now that scares me."

"I suggest we file a suit for defamation against Easton. Come out swinging."

"I like swinging."

30

Hot, soothing water sprayed on my skin as I scrubbed the whole experience away in the shower. I stayed in for way too long, thinking about how I would handle the situation.

When the hot water ran out, I stepped out of the steamy shower, toweled off, and got dressed.

"I feel like this is all my fault," Scarlett said as I stepped into the living room. "Maybe it was a mistake coming out here?"

"You didn't make a mistake. This is just a little bump in the road. I'll get things sorted out, I promise."

She sat on the couch, a somber frown tugging her lips.

A moment later, Sheriff Daniels called. "Am I to understand that you assaulted someone and threatened to kill them?"

"Lies and misunderstandings."

"That's not what LAPD says."

I grumbled under my breath, then gave Daniels a brief overview of the situation.

"You know, I have to put you on administrative leave while this is under investigation? This couldn't happen at a worse time. I'm leaving for Texas soon, and the Russell case is turning into a nightmare."

"What's going on?"

"You know the kid we brought in? Davon Jones. He's dead. Somebody stabbed him in the day-room with a shiv."

"Who?"

"Prison officials are reviewing the footage now to determine that."

I grimaced. "I get the feeling somebody didn't want him talking."

"I'm sure whoever he was hustling for was afraid he might rat them out," Daniels said. "I don't know if he killed Warren or not, but I want this thing sorted out, pronto. When are you coming back to Coconut Key?"

"I'll see if I can get a flight out today."

"Try to stay out of trouble," Daniels said before hanging up.

I called Isabella. I hated to ask for another favor, but she was my best option. As my former handler at *Cobra Company*, she had unmatched resources. "I need you to dig up dirt on Easton Carter."

"What kind of dirt?" Isabella asked.

"Anything that could be used as leverage." I told her about Easton's pattern of behavior and the situation with Scarlett.

"I'll find something," she assured. "But it's payback time."

"What do you need?"

"It's a simple job. Won't take much time, and you get to kill two birds with one stone."

"I'm listening."

"Relax. You'll like this. It will put you closer to Esteban Rivera."

I perked up. Esteban Rivera was indirectly responsible for my parents murder. Catching up with him was high on my priority list.

"Standard protection detail. I'll give you more info later."

Isabella hung up, and I made arrangements to return to Coconut Key.

Scarlett moped about the apartment. She seemed hopeless.

Joel called. "I've got bad news. Ari is on the line with me."

"Hello, Tyson," Ari said.

I knew when I heard his voice it wasn't going to be good.

Joel continued. "Seems like this is a bigger problem than I anticipated. It's all over the trades. Every industry website is covering it. The studio has lost interest in the TV show, and they are shelving the Bree Taylor project because of your association with it."

My jaw dropped. "Are you serious?"

"It gets worse," Joel said.

"How much worse?"

Ari took over. "There is a *morals clause* in your contract. If you do anything that can reflect negatively on the studio, you can be held liable for the repercussions. I would expect the studio to file suit soon. They'll be looking to recover damages."

"What damages?" I asked.

"The costs associated with developing the project," Ari said. "That means the advance they paid you, and any fees they paid to screenwriters that have worked on the project, plus other miscellaneous expenses."

"How can they do that?"

"Because it's in the contract which you signed."

"I thought you looked over the contract for me?"

"I did. But I didn't expect you to assault a power player in Hollywood."

I wanted to scream, but I contained my anger. My cheeks flushed with heat. "How much are we talking about?"

"The million dollar advance they paid you. The million dollars they paid the writer. Probably another 500,000 in miscellaneous expenses."

I swallowed hard. "They can file suit, but do you think they'll actually win?"

"Hard to say. You're in clear breach of contract. Anything can happen in a courtroom."

In the blink of an eye, I had gone from financially secure to flat broke if this lawsuit materialized.

31

After nearly 16 hours of travel, I was back in Coconut Key. Jack picked me up in the lizard-green Porsche, and I stuffed my suitcase in the tiny compartment that masqueraded as a trunk.

"What the hell is going on with you?" JD asked. "Daniels says you got suspended because you assaulted someone. What the hell were you doing out there?"

I figured I would have to come clean sooner or later. "Don't get mad."

"You go to Los Angeles, you get arrested, and you tell me not to get mad. Why do I feel like I'm gonna get mad when you tell me? You didn't..."

"No, I didn't," I said, knowing exactly what he was asking.

"If you're lying to me, I'll bust your ass."

I raised my hands, innocently.

Jack dropped the car into gear and lurched away from the

curb. The big orange ball that hung in the sky plummeted toward the horizon. The wind whipped through my hair as we raced across the island with the top down. I told him everything that had happened in LA while we drove back to the marina.

We pulled into the parking lot, and Jack stopped by the dock. The car idled, the flat six rumbling. Jack took a deep breath, and his eyes misted just slightly. "Shit, man. You'd do that for me?"

"You're family, Jack. Besides, you'd do the same for me."

"Damn straight!"

I told him about my legal troubles, and the fact that we might have to sell the boat.

JD scowled at me. "That boat's not going anywhere! I don't care how broke you end up."

I gave him an uncertain look.

"On the bright side, I've been doing some digging while you were gone," Jack said. "I interrogated the inmate that killed Davon Jones. He was sitting in a county holding unit waiting to be transferred to the penitentiary after getting handed a life sentence. Of course, he denied any involvement in the killing, despite the fact that he was caught on video. He's not saying a word, but I can almost guarantee he was hired to do it."

"That doesn't really get us anywhere."

"Just wait, there's more… I found out who Davon Jones was working for—mid-level dealer named Bam Bam."

I arched a curious eyebrow. *"Bam Bam?"*

"He's got several kids that work the streets for him. He's pretty savvy about his business. He's got these little punks on the street corners hustling. They carry just under the amount of a third-degree felony. That way if they get popped, the state has less leverage against them. When they have sold all their merchandise, they return to his stash house to resupply. The stash house is run by an underling, and Bam Bam never touches the operation. DEA has been trying to take the guy down for years. They can't get anything on him. He doesn't talk about it on the phone, or in text. In the grand scheme of things, he's relatively small time, so nobody has put an inordinate amount of effort into taking him down."

"So, Warren threatens his business model. Bam Bam orders Davon Jones to get rid of the problem. But Warren is dead when Davon arrives. So he says."

"This is where things get complicated," Jack said. "I think Davon is telling the truth. He couldn't have done it. There is security footage of him knocking off a convenience store at the time of the murder."

"So why was Davon shanked in prison?"

"I think Bam Bam was afraid the kid was gonna roll over."

I sighed. "So, who killed Warren?"

Jack shrugged. "I don't know." He paused. "Either way, Bam Bam needs to go down." A sparkle glimmered in Jack's eyes. "I gotta run. Plans with Sasha and Tasha."

"Who?" I asked.

"The roommates. They are teaching me to speak Russian!"

"This sounds like it's getting serious. How many times have you seen them?"

Jack shrugged and flashed a grin. "As often as I can."

I climbed out of the car and grabbed my roller-bag from under the hood. I waved as he peeled from the lot, then strolled into *Diver Down* and took a seat at the bar.

Harlan was in his usual spot.

"How was your trip?" Madison asked in a cheery tone.

"It was great." There was no sense in burdening her with my drama.

"Have you figured out who killed Warren yet?" Harlan asked.

I frowned. "Not yet. Getting closer."

"At this rate, I'm going to die of natural causes before you dingleberries figure it out. In the meantime, there are plenty of old folks on the island that are terrified."

I assured Harlan that the Sheriff's Department was on top of things.

It had been a long day of traveling, and my stomach rumbled. I ordered a cheeseburger and sweet potato fries, then washed it all down with a beer. Afterward, I collected Buddy and Fluffy, and strolled to the *Vivere*.

It was good to be home.

Buddy was excited to see me, and Fluffy didn't care.

I settled in, unpacked my suitcase, and poured a glass of whiskey. The events of the last few days filled my mind. I sure had gotten myself into a mess—one I wasn't sure I could get out of.

I went to the aft deck and took a seat on the lounge. Buddy climbed into my lap, and I stroked his fur. For a moment, he took away all of my stress. I sat there, enjoying the breeze, listening to the waves lap against the hull, sipping my whiskey.

When my glass was empty, I went back inside, took a shower, and climbed into bed. I watched a little TV, and an hour later, the phone rang as I was dozing off.

"You need to get to the hospital, ASAP," Denise said.

I sat up, eyes wide. "Why? What's wrong?"

32

"Somebody beat Jack with a crowbar," Denise said.

"What?" I exclaimed in disbelief.

"He got jumped in his driveway. Two girls found him. Sasha and Tasha. Do you know them?"

"They're Jack's Russian playthings."

"It's a good thing they found him when they did."

"Is he okay?"

"Not really. He's in a medically induced coma. I'm here with him at the Neurologic Intensive Care Unit. I heard the emergency dispatch come across the radio, and I came straight here."

"Why didn't you call me?"

"I'm calling you!"

"I'll see you there," I stammered.

The news hit me like a sledgehammer to the gut.

Buddy looked at me with sad eyes. He could tell something was wrong.

I grabbed my helmet and gloves and raced to the parking lot. I hopped on my Yamazuki X6, and the engine rattled as I cranked it up. I twisted the throttle and launched out of the parking lot, racing across town like a demon possessed. My heart pounded with nervous anticipation. In my mind, I imagined the worst.

My imagination wasn't far off.

I stormed into the ER and flashed my badge. "Looking for Jack Donovan in Neuro ICU?"

The receptionist pointed the way and gave me the room number.

I raced through the hallways to Jack's room.

Denise ran into my arms with wet eyes and gave me a hug. She was in her duty uniform.

Sasha and Tasha sat in chairs beside the bed with misty eyes and worried faces.

Jack had been beaten to a pulp.

He had multiple lacerations and bruises across his face and body. His skin was several shades of purple, yellow, blue, and red. A ventilator gasped and wheezed, breathing for Jack. Tubes were stuffed down his throat, and a feeding cannula went up his nose. He looked just barely this side of the living.

The monitor by the bed displayed vitals, and his heartbeat blipped, making craggy peaks on the screen.

I'd seen Jack in pretty bad shape before, but never anything like this. My throat tightened, and I scratched out the words, "How's he doing?"

"The doctor said he has severe brain trauma," Denise said. "They put him into a medically induced coma to reduce swelling, and they're inducing hypothermia to keep body temperature down which will help with swelling as well."

My stomach twisted. Seeing him like that was difficult. I swallowed hard, and a nervous sweat coated my body. My throat was so dry, I could hardly ask the question, "Is he going to make it?"

Denise bit her lip, then shrugged. A grim look washed over her face.

Rage boiled within me. I wanted to find who did this and put them in worse shape.

I re-introduced myself to the girls. We had met once on the boat. They wiped the tears from their eyes.

"Do you know who might have done this?" I asked.

The girls shook their heads.

"Jack was going to cook us dinner," Sasha said. "We found him when we walked up the driveway. He was on the ground beside his car. We called 911 right away."

"Did you see anyone in the area?"

They both shook their heads.

"I don't think this was a random mugging," Denise said. "Too violent."

"Jack had been looking into a local dealer named Bam Bam. I think this was a message to back off."

I stayed in the Neuro ICU with Jack for another hour, listening to the drone of the ventilator. I hesitated to call Scarlett. I didn't want to upset her, but I thought she might want to come back for a visit, just in case.

She burst into tears when I told her.

"I can get a flight out in the morning," Scarlett said. "It will probably be the evening before I get there. Please tell me he's going to be okay?"

"I hope so," I said. "There's nothing you can really do here."

"It doesn't matter. I'm coming! Can you pick me up from the airport?"

"Sure thing."

"I'll text you when I have my itinerary."

I hung up the phone, and the nurse came in to do a routine check. "You're more than welcome to stay here all night, but there's nothing you can do for him. I promise, he's in good hands, and we'll look after him."

Jack wasn't coming out of the medically induced coma anytime soon. And sitting in that room wasn't bringing me any closer to Jack's attacker, or Warren's killer.

I said goodbye to Sasha and Tasha, then Denise and I left the hospital and strolled to the parking lot.

News reporters swarmed us as we exited. Camera lights squinted my eyes, and microphones hovered overhead on boom poles.

"What can you tell us about the attack?" a reporter asked.

"Does this have anything to do with the Warren Russell murder?"

"Can you confirm the identity of the injured deputy?"

I extended my hand, stiff arming reporters as I pushed through the small crowd. "No comment at this time!"

An overhead light flickered, bathing the lot in long shadows. The reporters followed us as we strolled toward Denise's SUV. I climbed into the passenger seat so we could talk in private. The reporters hovered outside the windows, aiming their lenses inside. They kept shouting questions.

We tried to ignore them.

I grabbed a magazine from the floorboard and flattened it against the window, trying to obscure the cameras' view.

"What are you going to do?" Denise asked.

"Whatever I have to."

"You're still on leave. I can't technically discuss anything with you."

"You don't have to."

"Don't go do anything stupid," she said, staring into me. "I know how you are. You're not going to let this go."

"Damn right I'm not going to let this go!"

"And that's exactly what got you in trouble in Los Angeles."

I clenched my jaw.

"All I'm saying, is don't go take matters into your own hands.

I know how pissed off you are, but you need to go by the book."

"Right now *the book* has me on inactive status. I don't know how long it's going to take to square up this LA mess. You know how time-critical these cases can be."

"I will do everything I can. You know that," Denise said.

I nodded.

She leaned across the console and gave me a long, tight hug. I didn't want to let go of her.

When she broke away, her cheek brushed against mine. She lingered close, our lips inches apart. I could feel her sweet breath on my skin. Her fruity shampoo filled my nostrils. Heat radiated from her skin. For a moment, I forgot about the news reporters outside the vehicle.

Our lips inched toward each other on a collision course that had been inevitable since the moment I first set eyes on her. We were both in a heightened emotional state, and I needed something to comfort my soul. Denise could soothe my soul in spades.

Collision in 3...

2...

"Are you the deputy that was accused of assault in California?" a reporter shouted through glass, interrupting what could have been the most passionate kiss of my life.

I scowled at the reporter.

Denise pulled away and composed herself. "Jack's going to

be fine. Something like this isn't going to keep him down. He'll bounce back."

I wanted to believe it.

We stared at each other for a long, awkward moment.

"I should get home," Denise said.

I nodded, then pushed the door open and strolled across the parking lot to my bike. I pulled on my helmet, straddled the beast, and cranked up the engine. I waited for Denise to drive out of the parking lot before leaving. I twisted the throttle and cruised back to the marina.

Big Tony called as I strolled down the dock. "I saw on the news what happened to Jack. Is he going to be okay?"

I filled Tony in on the details. Tony knew just about everyone who was anyone in Coconut Key. His poker game was frequented by politicians, celebrities, drug dealers, tech millionaires, and anyone else with money to burn.

"You know a low-level dealer named *Bam Bam?*" I asked.

Tony growled. "Yeah. I know that guy."

"I take it you don't have anything good to say about him?"

"Just another one of these punks. No class. I had to kick him out of one of my games. Caught the bastard cheating." He paused for a moment. "Why do you ask? You think he may have had something to do with this?"

"It's possible, but... I don't know. If I had anything on him, I'd bring him in."

"Sit tight," Tony said with a growl. "I'll get back to you shortly."

He hung up the phone, and I strolled across the gangway to the aft deck of the *Vivere*. I wasn't sure what Tony was up to, but he sounded determined.

Buddy greeted me in the salon with a wagging tail. I knelt down and loved on the Jack Russell, then poured myself another glass of whiskey to unwind. Adrenaline coursed through my veins. Anger swelled within. I wanted to dispense swift justice. But there was no way for me to do that just yet.

33

"Meet me at *Major Third*," Tony said when he called back.

"Now?"

"Yes, now."

Major Third was an upscale jazz bar on Oyster Avenue. A gorgeous blonde in a red sequined dress clung to a retro microphone. Her hair was sculpted to perfection. She looked like a classic movie star. Her velvety voice filtered through the club, as a virtuoso tickled the keys behind her. The base was smooth and punchy, the guitar crisp and clean, and the drums snappy. The murmur of conversation floated in the air, and ice clinked in whiskey glasses.

I met Tony at the bar. The big guy leaned against the counter and had a glass of whiskey waiting for me.

"What's going on?" I asked.

"Just wait."

"For?"

"You'll see."

I took a sip of the amber liquid. It was smooth, top shelf stuff.

"Word has it he's a regular here," Tony said.

"Bam Bam?"

Tony nodded.

I leaned against the bar with Tony, sipping whiskey, taking in the sights and sounds of the club. When Bam Bam finally entered, he did so in style. He was impeccably dressed in an *Acardi* suit, a *Carboni* shirt, a *D'Antonio* silk tie and matching pocket square, and *Gaspari* leather cap-toe lace-up shoes. He had a gorgeous blonde on either arm. He was the picture of style and sophistication.

The hostess led him to a reserved table near the stage. A bottle of chilled champagne was quickly brought to him in a silver bucket of ice. The waiter popped the cork and poured the bubbly golden liquid into champagne flutes.

The ladies toasted their benefactor, and they sipped their drinks, leaving lipstick stains on the glasses. Bam Bam looked like he was in seventh heaven. And who wouldn't be? It seemed like he had it all.

"He's here every night till close." Tony said. "He always sits at that table."

"Great. But I can't arrest him for listening to jazz music."

"Who said anything about arresting him?" Tony muttered.

I'm not sure exactly what he had in mind, but it probably wasn't legal.

"You can't tell me that guy doesn't have an eight ball in his pocket," Tony said.

"You want me to bust him on a bullshit possession charge? Then what?"

"You lean on him a little."

"I can lean on him all I want, but he's not going to come out and say he ordered one of his thugs to kill Warren or beat up Jack."

Tony smiled. "I was hoping you'd come to that conclusion."

"Even if I could to bring him in, I'm on leave."

There was a long pause, then Tony chose his words carefully. "I'm not suggesting anything, mind you. But you could grab him and bag him. Waterboard him until the son-of-a-bitch talks."

"Oh, sure. Why not?" I said, my voice thick with sarcasm. "I'm not in enough trouble. Let's add more."

"That scumbag had Jack put into the hospital. He probably had the old man killed. And what happens the next time somebody tries to get one of his pushers to stop dealing around the schools? You think this is just going to stop?"

I knew Tony was right, but I didn't like where this was going.

"How many kids are going to die because of the shit he puts on the street? And what happens when he starts cutting his product with fentanyl, or something worse?"

I hadn't seen Tony get this worked up since his daughter was kidnapped.

"Look, I'm no angel. But I've got a soft spot for kids, old people, and animals. This scumbag needs to go down."

I gritted my teeth. "So, what's your plan?"

A sly grin curled on Tony's lips. He subtly motioned to the table next to Bam Bam.

Two men sat with stoic faces, surveying the crowd, monitoring the entrances and exits. They weren't interested in the show. While Bam Bam was enjoying himself, his hired guns were all business.

"That's his security. They carry pistols in shoulder holsters, and subcompacts around the ankles. That's the only security he has. We can take them down easy peasy."

My eyes narrowed at Tony. "You're a bad influence."

He shrugged innocently. "Who me?"

We stayed at the club for the rest of the evening and observed Bam Bam. After the club closed, we followed him and his entourage to an after-hours bar where he stayed until 3 AM, before heading home.

I rode in the passenger seat of Tony's car as we tailed them through the streets of the city. Bam Bam's SUV pulled up to a luxurious home which backed up to a canal. It was a three-story mansion. Palm trees out front swayed with the breeze.

A security guard hopped out of the passenger seat and opened the back door for Bam Bam and his companions. They slid out of the plush leather seats, and the driver killed the engine. He hopped out of the driver's side, observed the surroundings, then followed the entourage to the front door.

The bodyguard led the way. He opened the front door, advancing into the home, clearing the area.

Bam Bam entered with the blondes.

The driver scanned the yard again, then entered behind them.

Bam Bam wasn't taking any chances. Every drug dealer had rivals. When you got to a certain level, everybody was trying to knock you off. Rivals either wanted your territory, or they needed bragging rights and street credibility. Survival of the most ruthless.

Tony grinned. "Like I said, this is easy. Take out the two security guards. Snatch the wanna-be kingpin. We leave the girls screaming."

"Then what?"

"You get some answers."

"And if he admits to ordering the death of Warren?"

Tony shrugged. "You can save the tax payers some money."

This was exactly the type of thing I was avoiding.

I was no stranger to this type of operation. There were many times during my clandestine career when we had to snatch an enemy leader, or a member of an opposition party, and extract information. Once the asset was *depleted*, they were often *retired*.

It wasn't like fishing. You couldn't just catch and release. Any secrets you may have acquired from the *asset* became useless if the breach of security became revealed to the enemy. I had dispatched plenty of depleted assets in my day. I had always told myself it was for a good and just cause.

Tony could sense my hesitation. "He put your friend into a coma. Are you going to let that slide?"

Bam Bam was a bad man. But kidnapping him, torturing him, and killing him wasn't exactly going to earn me any brownie points in my quest for redemption.

"Sometimes you gotta get a little dirty to clean things up," Tony said.

I thought for another moment. "This is a three person job. We need a wheel-man and two operators."

Tony grinned. "Relax. It's all taken care of. I've already made some phone calls. Go home. I'll call you when it's done."

I gave him a curious glance.

"You did me a solid. I'm returning the favor. Now I'm gonna take you home. Plausible deniability, and all that. In case things go wrong."

34

I didn't get much sleep. My mind raced. To say I had misgivings about this whole operation would be an understatement. There was a line that I had been trying not to cross, but I kept finding myself on the other side of it.

It was just before sunrise when Tony called. My cabin was still pitch black. I grabbed the phone and swiped the screen. My brain could barely form sentences, and my raspy morning voice filed a workplace grievance. "Is it done?"

"Rise and shine, sleepyhead," Tony said in that thick New York accent. "I don't know anything about this, mind you. But I just got an *anonymous* phone call. There is a gift-wrapped package for you in the abandoned warehouse by *Salt Point Harbor.*"

I was silent a moment.

"Say *thank you, Tony.*"

"Thank you, Tony," I said, my voice still scratchy.

I hung up the phone and climbed out of bed. I pulled on a pair of shorts, a T-shirt, and stuffed my holster inside my waistband for an appendix carry. There was no time for breakfast.

I left the boat and jogged down the dock to my bike. A moment later, I was cruising down the highway, the wind whistling through my helmet.

There was an old red brick warehouse by the harbor with hazy windows, most of them busted. It had been many things over the years, but had sat empty for the last several. It needed a major renovation. There was probably asbestos in the insulation around the piping and in the floor tiles. The renovation would probably cost more than the property itself. Then there were the demolition permits. The large for sale sign on the side of the building was faded and stressed.

I rode my bike into the empty parking lot. The main doors were locked, and the first story windows were mostly boarded shut—except for one that had been ripped away during the last storm. The transom window was ajar.

I spread it farther open with a squeak, then grabbed the sill and pulled myself through the narrow space.

I tumbled into the dusty warehouse. Shafts of morning light beamed in, illuminating the hazy air. Paint was flaking and cracked. Old invoices were scattered about the floor. The cavernous space was mostly empty, save for a few pieces of machinery. In the middle of the room was my prize.

Bam Bam was tied to a chair with a black bag over his head. He wore gold silk underwear, and gold socks. That was it.

He'd been snatched from his bed in the wee hours of the

morning by Tony's *associates*. His Mafia connections could get to anybody.

Near Bam Bam, on the floor, was a self-striking, trigger activated, propane torch. It had a removable propane canister the size of a can of spray paint. You could purchase one at any home improvement store. A yellow sticky note attached to the torch read: *Truth Serum.*

Beside the torch was a pair of pliers. Next to that was a ball-peen hammer. Tony had thought of everything.

Bam Bam heard me shuffle through the cavernous space, unable to see. He stammered, "You back for more?"

"Tell me about Davon Jones?"

"Man, I don't know no Davon Jones!"

Bloodstains seeped through the black bag over his head. He'd been worked over pretty good before I got to him.

"That's not the answer I want to hear."

"Who are you? What do you want?"

"I just told you what I want. I want you to start telling the truth, or things are going to get really ugly for you."

"Man, go fuck yourself."

I couldn't resist the urge to pummel the scumbag in the face. I threw a right cross that connected with his cheek and wrenched his head to the side.

Damn, that felt good!

It hurt my knuckles, but it felt good.

Bam Bam groaned.

"You can drop the tough guy act," I said. "It's not working for you."

"I guarantee, you are going to pay. When I get out of here, my crew is going to fuck you up."

I laughed. "Really? *Your crew?* Let's see, would that be the same *crew* that kept you from getting kidnapped in the middle of the night?"

Bam Bam was silent.

"Oh, that's right, they didn't. So now you're here. And if you want to walk out of this warehouse alive, you're going to tell me everything I want to know." I was bluffing—I think.

"Who are you?"

"Your worst nightmare. Let me give you a little bit of background... I'm extremely well trained in interrogation tactics. I also know my way around anatomy. I have plenty of experience with torture. And I don't get squeamish. I'm thinking about starting with a pair of pliers. I'll pull out your fingernails one by one, and I guarantee you, by the time I get to 10, you won't want to stop talking."

Bam Bam trembled slightly.

"Maybe I'll take a ball-peen hammer to the toes. That's always fun. After that, I've got a propane blowtorch. I like using those on the eyes. If you heat them just right, they'll boil and pop. Excruciating."

"Alright, alright! What the fuck do you want to know?"

"Tell me about Davon Jones?"

I scooped up the propane torch and ignited it. Bam Bam heard the strike of the flint and the ignition of the gas. Blue flame spewed from the nozzle. I held it in front of his face so he could feel the heat.

"Nothing to tell," Bam Bam said. "Davon slings product for me."

"You mean, he used to."

"Yeah, he's dead. Tragedy."

"Did you order the hit?"

Bam Bam said nothing.

I inched the blue flame closer.

He leaned his head as far away as he could. I kept moving the blue flame closer to the black bag.

"Okay. Shit, man! Yeah, I ordered the hit. He was gonna roll on me. They had him on murder charges."

"Which brings me to my next question. Did you send him to kill the old man?"

"What old man?"

"Warren Russell?"

"Yeah. So what?"

"That man was a goddamn hero!"

"Why do you give a shit?"

I growled at him and pushed the flame even closer. "Because I do."

"Ease up, bro. The old man was dead when Davon got to him. Somebody else killed him."

"Who?"

"How the fuck should I know?"

"The cop that was assaulted last night. One of your men do that?"

"What are you talking about?"

I jammed the blue flame millimeters from his right eye.

Bam Bam twisted his head away.

"The deputy that's been sniffing around asking questions about you. You didn't put a hit on him?"

"Oh, man. I didn't even know I was under investigation."

"Are you lying to me?" I asked, continuing to threaten him with the flame.

"Motherfucker, why would I lie?"

I pulled the flame away and extinguished it. I snatched the pliers from the ground and snapped them twice. "I think I'll save the seared eyeballs for later and start with the fingernails. How does that sound?"

"I swear to God, I'm not lying! That's the God's honest truth."

I let him stew in his own panic for a moment. "What are you willing to do to avoid torture and disfigurement?"

"Anything. You name it." He paused. "I mean, you don't want me to suck nothing, do you?"

"Let me tell you how this is gonna go down. I'm gonna call

the cops. They're gonna find you here. You're going to confess to contracting the murder of Davon Jones. You're going to spill the beans on your little drug operation. Is that clear?"

Ban Bam nodded.

"If you don't, I'll come after you. You know I can get you anywhere. And I will make you regret it." I snapped the pliers twice again.

Bam Bam flinched.

"Are we clear?"

"We're clear."

I left the warehouse and crawled out the window, then called Denise. "Hey, I got an anonymous tip that a drug dealer was tied up in a warehouse. Can you send a patrol unit to check out the old warehouse near *Salt Point Harbor?*"

"An anonymous tip, eh?" she asked, full of skepticism.

35

I was back to square one with nothing to go on. All of my leads washed out.

I dreaded my next call, but I told Haley I'd keep her informed. I was about to dial her number when she called first. "Hey, is that your friend, Jack, that was attacked? I just saw on the news. Is he okay?"

"He's in critical, but stable condition."

"Oh, my God. That's terrible. Is he going to be okay?"

"That's anybody's guess right now. But, the doctors are optimistic."

"Do you think it is connected to my grandfather's case?"

"I think so."

"I was going through boxes of Warren's papers, and I found something curious. Do you have time to come over and take a look?"

"Sure, I'll be right there."

I hung up the phone and zipped over to Warren's house. I parked the bike at the curb and strolled to the front door. Haley heard me pull up and was waiting in the doorway.

"It might be nothing, or it might be something," she said.

I followed her through the house to the kitchen where she had a stack of papers on the breakfast table.

"These are photographs of medical records from patients at the assisted living facility. It looks like Pappy took pictures on his cell phone, then printed them out. There are stacks and stacks of them."

I looked over the records which included invoices and billing statements.

"Look at these charges." She pointed to one of the statements. "It's outrageous. Just about every one of these patients was given a specific genetic test to diagnose a condition that they didn't have. Medicare was billed $16,000 for this test." She flipped through the pages. "Here it is again, and again, and again. They billed $1900 for a walker. $795 for a toilet seat riser. $4500 for a knee brace. $5400 for a back brace." Haley flipped through a few more pages. "This woman was billed for a CAT scan, MRI, x-rays, 3D CT scan, and a musculoskeletal ultrasound, all in one week."

My eyes widened at the amount of some of these charges.

"That facility is committing Medicare fraud. They are most likely prescribing devices that aren't medically necessary, and perhaps weren't even provided. I think Pappy found out, and they killed him." She looked at me with terrified eyes. "I know it sounds crazy, but—"

"You don't have to convince me. I agree. He must have sneaked into the office and photographed all these records."

"I checked his phone records," Haley said. "He made several phone calls to the state regulator."

"And nothing happened," I said. I stood there for a moment, processing the information. "Have you told anyone else about this?"

Haley shook her head.

"I don't think it's safe for you to stay here anymore."

"I'm with you on that one."

"We'll load these records into your car. I've got a guest room on the boat, or we can take you over to the *Seven Seas*. Wherever you'd feel safer."

"You've got a gun, so I'm sticking with you."

I put the papers back in the bankers box and grabbed it by the cut out handles.

"My car is in the driveway," Haley said. She rushed ahead of me and pulled open the back door.

I stepped outside, then rounded the corner to the driveway. That's when a glimmering blade slashed toward me.

I blocked the knife with the box. The blade stabbed through the cardboard and into the stack of papers. I shoved the box against the attacker, driving him into Haley's SUV.

He slammed against the door and bent the mirror.

The box tumbled away, and papers went flying. The wind carried them in all directions.

The guy wielding the knife wore a black ski mask, black shirt, and black pants. He pushed off the car and lunged toward me swinging the shiny blade.

I drew my pistol, took aim, and squeezed off two rounds. The 9mm hammered against my palm, and smoke wafted from the barrel. The two bullets slammed into the man's chest with a thunk. The blast knocked him back against the car, and he slid down the quater panel. The knife fell from his hand as his grip went slack. He coughed and choked and spit blood from his mouth. His hands clutched at the gaping wound in his chest, but he couldn't stem the tide.

After a moment, his eyes went blank, and he slumped. The last of his blood oozed from the pits of flesh in his chest.

I moved close, kicked the knife away, then felt for a pulse in his neck.

His heart had been turned into ground beef. Pulverized by the 9mm hollow points. There was no doubt about it—he was dead.

The whole thing happened in the blink of an eye, and Haley looked on in horror. Frozen at the back door, with wide eyes and pale skin.

I pulled off the man's ski mask. I didn't recognize his face. With my cell phone, I took a picture and texted it to Isabella. I knew she would be able to run the image through a facial recognition database and come up with a name.

Haley started to gather up the papers that were dancing on the wind.

I called Denise and told her what transpired. Before long, the area was forming with patrol cars and emergency vehicles. Red and blue lights flickered. A crowd of neighbors gathered around.

The news crews weren't far behind.

Daniels stormed onto the scene with a scowl on his face. He looked at the dead body, then his hard eyes glanced to me. "What part of *administrative leave* do you not understand?"

I shrugged. "I was here on personal business."

His eyes narrowed. He didn't buy it for one second.

36

"You know that guy you arrested for video voyeurism? Zeke?" Denise said, poking her head into Daniels's office.

I sat across the desk from Daniels, explaining our theory, showing him Warren's photos, and listening to him rant.

Haley sat beside me.

"Yeah, what about him?" I asked.

"Well, he wants to make a deal."

"So?" Daniels grumbled.

"He says he's got footage of a local doctor hiring a hitman to kill Warren. It's the same man that attacked Tyson. Wants the charges dropped in exchange. The DA is reviewing the footage now. And Zeke has been put in protective custody."

"I want to see that footage ASAP," Daniels growled.

"I'm on it," Denise said, then pulled the door closed as she left.

"My contact got an ID on the hitman," I said. "He is a freelancer from New York. I can almost guarantee you that the doctor who hired him is the same one who signed off on these fraudulent procedures. Dr. Gardner."

Daniels frowned. "And I was just about to move my dad into that place." He paused for a moment. "This is big. If what you say is true, and Warren did call the state regulator, there's no telling how deep this fraud goes. I'm going to contact the FBI, Department of Justice, Health and Human Services, and anybody else I can think of. We'll put together a joint task force and bust this thing wide open."

I liked the sound of that.

Daniels pointed at me. "But you! You stay out of this. Worry about your own legal troubles right now."

A frown twisted on my face. I didn't like sitting back and watching from the sidelines. Maybe I was just an adrenaline junkie?

Haley and I left Sheriff Daniels's office. We strolled through the busy department, and Denise waved me over to her desk.

"I got the footage from the DA. He sent a link." She pulled it up on her computer screen and we watched the high-definition footage.

The man who attacked me had a conversation in a hotel room at the *Seven Seas* with Dr. Gardner—the same doctor that attended to Eugene when we visited the C-KALF. He had the same perfect smile, square jaw, and dark hair. He handed the hitman a duffel bag full of money.

"I need you to make it look like an accident, or a burglary," Gardner said.

"No problem," replied the hitman, sifting through the cash.

"I need you to search the house. He knows details about our operation. We've got surveillance footage of him in the office making copies of billing statements and invoices. Find those." Gardner paused. "You don't have any problem killing the elderly, do you?"

The hitman looked at him flatly. "It's all the same to me."

"His name is Warren Russell."

That was all I needed to see. My blood boiled. I sure was jealous I was going to miss out on the action. I wanted to see that scumbag's face when they slapped the cuffs on his wrists.

Haley watch the video, tears streaming down her cheeks.

Denise handed her a tissue, and she wiped the moisture away from her red, puffy eyes. "How can people be so cruel?"

I put my arm around her and tried to comfort her. "Don't worry. Gardner is going to pay. One way, or another."

We left the station, and Haley followed me back to *Diver Down*. She said she would feel more comfortable staying on the boat with me until this whole thing was wrapped up.

"Wow, this is a really nice boat," she said as we strolled down the dock.

"Better enjoy it while it lasts. I don't think it's going to be around for long."

Her face crinkled with curiosity.

"Long story. Cash flow is about to be a problem."

She frowned. "I'm sorry to hear that."

We crossed the gangway and stepped into the salon. Buddy bounced up and down like a maniac, barking. Haley knelt down and petted him, and the little Jack Russell instantly melted her heart.

He had a way of doing that.

I gave her a tour the boat and showed her to the VIP guest suite. "I really appreciate this. This is very kind of you. I can't thank you enough for everything you've done for me, and for Warren."

"It's my pleasure. I'm just glad we were able to figure this thing out."

"I'd like to go to the hospital and see your friend Jack."

"I've got to pick up Jack's daughter from the airport this afternoon. But I figured we'd swing by the hospital on the way back. You're welcome to join, if you'd like."

Haley nodded.

"Are you hungry?"

"Starving."

We strolled to *Diver Down* and took a seat at the bar. I introduced her to Madison and Harlan, and we ate lunch. Afterward, we had a little time to kill, so we strolled back to the boat.

There was a man waiting on the dock by the *Vivere*, holding an envelope. "Tyson Wild?"

I hesitated to answer. Anytime someone needed to identify me before speaking, I figured it was bad news.

37

The man handed me an envelope, and said, "You've been served."

I clenched my jaw, and my fist tightened around the envelope.

The man scurried away quickly.

I tore open the bad news. It was a notice of a wrongful death suit brought by the hitman's family.

I wanted to scream.

The guy attacks me, kills countless others, and I'm the one who get sued?

"That's total bullshit," Haley said.

We boarded the boat. I crumpled up the notice and threw it in the trash. "I don't know about you, but I could use a drink."

A thin smile tugged her plump lips.

"I've got whiskey, beer, and rum?"

"I'll have what you're having."

I stepped into the salon and went straight for the whiskey. I poured two glasses, then returned to the aft deck. We took a seat in the lounge.

I lifted my glass, "To Warren."

Haley smiled. "To Warren."

We clinked glasses, and I sipped the smooth whiskey.

I looked out over the water, tried to let all of my troubles melt away. Nothing was certain. I didn't know if Jack would make it. I didn't know how much longer I would be able to call the *Vivere* home.

There were a lot of things in flux.

Worrying wouldn't change the outcome of anything. I tried to detach from it all and just live in the moment.

"You never told me what you did for a living?" I asked.

"Don't laugh. I write steamy romance novels."

"Really?"

"Yeah, I can do it anywhere. As long as I have a laptop or an iPad."

"That's great. I'd love to read some of your work."

"They get pretty dirty," she said with a naughty grin.

"I can handle dirty."

"After this experience, I may start writing mysteries."

We shared a laugh.

Later that afternoon, we picked up Scarlett from the airport. She greeted me with a hug and terrified eyes. I introduced her to Haley, and we zipped over to the hospital. Scarlett burst into tears as she stepped into the Neuro ICU and saw Jack.

He was barely recognizable.

Scarlett moved to the bed and held Jack's hand. The ventilator wheezed, and his heartbeat blipped on the monitor.

Scarlett struggled to hold back the tears. "Dad. It's me, Scarlett," she whispered, taking his hand.

She waited for a sign, a slight squeeze of the hand, a grunt—anything to acknowledge her presence.

Jack didn't respond.

Scarlett's eyes filled again, and she sobbed. "You're going to be okay, Dad. I know it. Just hang in there. Please be okay!" she pleaded.

It was hard to watch. A lump grew in my throat, and an elephant stepped on my chest. I put my arm around Scarlett and said, "He'll pull through. Not even cockroaches can outlive Jack."

Scarlett said she would stay at the hospital the entire night. She wouldn't leave Jack's side. Haley and I brought her dinner from the cafeteria before leaving, and I told her to call me if she needed anything during the night.

We headed back to the *Vivere*. I took Buddy for a run, then settled in for the evening.

In the morning, the FBI, along with the Sheriff's Department, and Health and Human Services Office of Inspector General raided C-KALF. All of their computers, hard drives, and records were confiscated. The general manager, Todd, was arrested along with several members of the staff.

Dr. Gardner was still at large.

It would take several weeks to sort through the whole scheme. The network of corruption had spread to the hospital that referred patients, and the state regulator who overlooked complaints. It was one of the largest busts in the state's history with estimates as high as $72 million in fraudulent billing. Todd and Dr. Gardner had made a not so small fortune.

I watched the evening news coverage on TV as I sat in the bar at *Diver Down*. Emma Steele broke the story. A picture of Gardner flashed on the screen. "And the doctor responsible for it all is still at large. If you have any information on the whereabouts of this man, please contact the Coconut County Sheriff's Department, or your local FBI office, immediately."

The phone number for the FBI and the Sheriff's Department flashed on the screen.

"You're slipping, Tyson," Harlan said. "You don't usually leave loose ends."

"It's not over, yet," I assured.

"Where do you think Gardner is?" Haley asked.

"I don't know. He's looking at multiple counts. Conspiracy to commit murder. Medicare fraud. When they catch him, he's going away for a long time."

"This isn't going to feel resolved if he gets away," Haley said.

"He's not going to get away if I have anything to say about it."

I relied on Isabella once again. As much as I hated to keep asking favors from her, I had no choice. When we spoke, I laid it on thick. "It's for a good cause. You'll sleep easier knowing you helped get one more scumbag off the street."

"What do you need?" she asked.

"Track a cell phone. Tell me if the perp has any offshore bank accounts. Any property in his name. If I were Gardner, I'd be getting out of the country as fast as possible. Let me know if he turns up anywhere."

"Will do," Isabella said. She paused. "By the way, I'm still working on your situation in Los Angeles."

"I appreciate that."

"I'll let you know what I find out." Isabella hung up.

We ate at the bar, and I ordered a cheeseburger to go, for Scarlett. Afterward, Haley and I headed up to the hospital to bring Scarlett dinner and see Jack.

To my surprise, Jordyn was sitting in the room with Scarlett.

"What are you doing here?" I asked.

"Can't a girl see a friend in the hospital?" Jordyn replied.

"I didn't think you cared," I said.

She huffed. "I may be a little wild, but I have a heart. I had fun partying with you guys. I mean, before I made an ass out of myself."

"So, you're admitting to making an ass out of yourself?"

"I'll admit when I screw up." She sighed. "I guess I kind of, sort of, owe you an apology."

"*Kind of?*"

"I shouldn't have called you an asshole the other day at *Wetsuit*. You were just trying to diffuse the situation."

I gave her a skeptical glance.

"I'll be cool now. I promise! Do you still hate me?"

She made a pouty face and tried to look innocent. Of course she bounced slightly, jiggling her breasts for added encouragement.

"I guess we are cool now," I said.

"Yay!" Jordyn jumped up and down, bobbling in delightful ways.

"Jordyn's going to come see me in Los Angeles. We're going to have so much fun," Scarlett said.

"Oh, no you're not."

Scarlett scowled at me.

"Don't be a party pooper," Jordyn said.

I gave Jordyn a stern look. "You are a bad influence. Do not corrupt her."

Jordyn rolled her eyes. "I can't corrupt anyone who doesn't want to be corrupted."

"Why don't you put your charms to good use and go talk dirty into JD's ear? That might initiate a healing response."

"Sugar, I can make a dead man walk," Jordyn said with a devious sparkle.

She sauntered over to the bed, leaned over the rail, and whispered something in Jack's ear.

Maybe it was just my imagination, but his pulse increased slightly.

After a moment she sauntered back in my direction. "Oh, I forgot to tell you. That doctor guy that you are looking for. I think I may know where he is."

38

"We kind of hooked up once," Jordyn said.

"When?" I asked.

"Maybe a month ago? He's got a really nice boat. Not as nice as yours. Yours is a little... bigger." Her pupils dilated. "Anyway, we went on a little booze cruise. He took me to this little island. It was a nice place. He said a friend of his owned it. Maybe that's where he is hiding out?"

"Do you remember where this island is?"

Jordyn shrugged. "I don't know. I was pretty wasted."

"How far away was it?"

Jordyn shrugged. "Maybe an hour? I don't know."

"Did you travel south, east, north?"

She looked at me flatly. "Sweetie, do I look like I would have any idea?"

"Grouper Key? Tarpon Key, Stone key?

"None of those." She frowned.

"Deadwood Key?"

Her eyes brightened. "Yeah. That's it."

"Are you sure?"

"Positive. Sort of. I don't know."

"You're not helping."

She shrugged. "I'm sorry. I'm trying. I'm not good with this kind of thing."

"Would you recognize the place if you saw it again?"

"Absolutely," Jordyn said.

"Then you're coming with me."

"What are you going to do?" Haley asked.

"We're just going on an exploratory mission. We'll visit the island and see if Gardner is there."

"And if he is?" Haley asked.

"We'll notify the authorities," I said.

Haley gave me a skeptical glance.

"Trust me. I'm in enough trouble already."

"I'm going with you," Haley said.

I sighed. "Okay. But both of you have to do exactly as I say. Stay on the boat at all times. And call for backup if there's any trouble."

"I'm going too," Scarlett said.

My face crinkled at her. "No, you're not. Stay here with Jack."

"Tyson!" she protested.

"End of discussion."

She frowned at me and folded her arms, sitting back in the chair. "You're no fun."

We left the hospital and headed back to the marina. Jordyn sat in the backseat of the SUV and leaned forward between the two front seats with an excited grin on her face. "This is going to be so awesome. I feel like a spy or something."

I rolled my eyes. "You are not a spy. You're just going to identify the island and see if Gardner's boat is there."

"I know how to fire a gun," Jordyn said.

"Oh, really?" I asked, doubtful.

"I did this cheesy B-movie once, *Bikini Beach Bimbos Save the World*. We ran around the whole time with machine guns, fighting really bad CG dinosaurs."

I flashed her a doubtful glance. "That doesn't make you a weapons expert."

"There was some former military guy on set that taught us how to handle the weapons and shoot. They took us to the range and let us fire off a few rounds before filming."

"I didn't know you were into acting," I said.

"I'm not. They filmed it in Miami a couple years ago. A friend of mine was doing make up on set, and the director saw me and said that I *had* to be in the movie." Jordyn smiled. "It's really bad."

"I'm pretty good with a rifle myself," Haley said. "You don't think a former Marine would let his granddaughter grow up without the ability to handle a firearm, do you?"

I grinned. "Good to know."

Haley pulled into the parking lot at *Diver Down* and parked the car. We jogged down the dock and boarded the *Vivere*. The girls played with Buddy as I prepped my gear. I press checked my pistol, gathered my assault rifle, extra magazines, night vision goggles, smoke grenades, and anything else I thought I might need for a tactical assault.

Jordyn looked on with wide eyes. "Holy shit! You've got a fucking arsenal. You could invade a small nation with this stuff."

"That's the idea," I said with a grin.

Haley and Jordyn disconnected shore power and water and cast off the lines. I idled the *Vivere* out of the marina and into the open water. Running full out, it took us about an hour to get to Deadwood Key.

I cut the lights and killed the engine and drifted about a 1/2 mile offshore. I dropped anchor, and the *Vivere* hovered in the inky blackness.

With a pair of binoculars, I scanned the island. It was a small key, maybe three quarters of a mile long and half a mile wide. There was an elevated home on the island, and I could see a few lights were on.

A channel had been dredged out to accommodate larger boats at the dock. The island was thick with mangrove trees and a few palms and high grass. It was a perfect secluded getaway.

A 45' sport fish was docked at the pier.

"Do you recognize that boat?" I asked Jordyn.

She shook her head. "That's not Gardner's."

I frowned.

I donned my tactical vest and helmet and slung my rifle over my shoulder.

"Where are you going?" Haley asked.

"To find out if Gardner was here, and where he went."

"Don't you need a warrant for that kind of thing?" Haley asked.

"I'm just going to have a friendly conversation." I smiled.

Haley arched a doubtful eyebrow at me. "What do you want us to do?"

"Stay here." I handed her the binoculars. "Keep an eye out. If I get into trouble, call for help."

She swallowed hard. "What kind of trouble?"

"Don't worry. Everything is going to be fine."

I descended the aft steps, lowered the swim platform, and launched the tender. I cast off the lines and twisted the throttle on the electric barracuda motor. The rigid inflatable plowed toward the island.

The new Barracuda electric motor was more powerful than the old Barracuda we had in the previous tender, but it wasn't going to win any races.

I circled the boat around the island, scoping out the terrain, then I headed to shore. I hopped out in the shallows and pulled the boat up the beach to the tree line. From a pocket, I grabbed a black balaclava and pulled it over my head, obscuring my face. Then I put on my helmet and lowered my NODs (night optical device). Like a jungle cat, I advanced through the trees, weaving through the underbrush to the house.

A man and a woman were inside, drinking wine. The guy was early 40s. The girl looked to be late 20s. She was cute. The guy—not so much. But he had more than enough money and toys to entertain her.

The pretty brunette leaned over the counter and sniffed a white powdery substance through a straw. She had a nice *lean*. She wore a skintight black dress with a high hemline that accentuated her toned legs. Afterward, she stood up, flipped her hair back, sniffled, and wiped her nose.

She handed the straw to the man. He snorted another line.

Upon witnessing that, I didn't feel so bad about kicking down the door.

39

Wood splintered from the doorjamb as I kicked my way into the house. I entered with my weapon in the firing position amid shrieks and hollers. "Get down on the ground! Facedown!"

With terrified eyes, they complied.

"Please, don't hurt us!" the man said. "You can take anything you want."

I could only imagine what the man must have been feeling. To be completely wired when a home invader stormed in with an assault rifle, barking commands? That's the stuff of nightmares.

He trembled on the floor.

"Where is Gardner?" I asked.

"Who?"

"Don't play games with me," I growled. "Where is he?"

"I don't know."

"Bullshit."

"I swear. I don't know," he stammered.

"Say *I don't know* one more time. I dare you."

"He's not here," the man said. "You're too late. He's already gone."

"Where?"

"Who are you?"

"A guy who's going to put a bullet in your skull if you don't start telling me what I want to know."

"Man, I swore I wouldn't say anything."

"Looks like you're about to break your promise. Where is he?"

He was silent a moment. Sweat sprouted on his forehead. He finally blurted, "He took his boat to Cuba. That's all I know."

"Where in Cuba?"

He hesitated. "Havana."

I nudged the barrel of my weapon closer.

"He's at the Hotel Castillo," the man said.

"If you're lying to me..."

"I swear to God, man. I'm telling you the truth. Gardner's an old friend from high school. He needed a place to stay. I didn't know what he was into. I don't have anything to do with his business."

"For your sake, I hope not." I paused. "If I find that you're lying to me, I'll be back. And you won't like it."

"I don't like it as it is."

I backed out of the kitchen, exited the house, and disappeared back into the underbrush. I raced through the trees to the tender, dragged it into the surf, and climbed aboard. I twisted the throttle, and the little electric outboard propelled me across the black water.

Jordyn and Haley waited on the aft deck. When I reached the swim platform, Haley engaged the hydraulic lift. I climbed out of the tender and secured it before ascending the steps to join them.

"Was Gardner there?" Haley asked.

I shook my head.

"Did you find out where he went?"

"Havana."

Haley's face tensed. "There's no extradition from Cuba. He's as good as gone."

A staggering number of criminals had fled to Cuba over the years and escaped prosecution in the United States. Cuba seemed to welcome anyone that pissed off the US government. Many fugitives lived the rest of their days, enjoying an unrestricted life. There were several fugitives in Cuba that had a high bounty on their heads. Some were worth upwards of $2 million. The idea flashed in my head that if my financial situation got really tight, maybe I'd get into the bounty hunter business?

Haley looked dejected. She exhaled, and her body slumped.

"Trust me. I'm not going to let that scumbag get away with this. I'll find him."

I moved to the helm, cranked up the engines, and headed us back to Coconut Key.

Jordyn slinked beside me at the helm. She looked up at me with big, apologetic eyes. She had an adorably pouty look on her face. "So, are we all square, daddy?"

"We're square," I said.

"And you're not still mad at me?"

"I'm not mad at you," I assured.

A bright smile curled on her full lips. "Yay!"

She gave me a big hug and squeezed tight. "This was fun. I want to do more spy shit. I could totally go undercover whenever you need me to." She arched a seductive eyebrow, and there was a hint of a double entendre in her words. "I think I'd be a good spy. I could totally infiltrate the enemy. Seduce the opposition. Expose their weaknesses."

"Maybe you missed your calling in life?" I joked.

"I'm young. And it's not too late."

I chuckled.

Haley watched the exchange and rolled her eyes.

I idled the boat into the marina, and we tied off and reconnected shore power and water. The night was still young, and Jordyn suggested we all go for a drink. She was in the mood to party.

I was in the mood to get to Havana.

40

"Gardner is definitely in Havana," Isabella said. "Looks like he's got a numbered offshore account in the Cayman Islands. He used a burner phone to access that account using the Wi-Fi at the Hotel Castillo less than an hour ago. He's got access to cash, and no extradition treaty. He could probably live the rest of his life in Havana like a king."

"I'll make sure that doesn't happen," I said.

"What's your plan?"

"I'm sure with your connections, you could pull some strings at the OFAC (Office of Foreign Asset Control) and get me a license."

"Anything else?" she asked with a healthy dose of sarcasm.

"I'll need a cover ID, a *Go Fast* boat, and a driver."

"Seriously?"

"I'll make it up to you. I promise."

She paused for a moment. "Are you going down there to bring him back? Or make him disappear?"

"I haven't decided yet."

"Customs will search the boat when you arrive. You won't be able to bring a weapon into the country."

"I'll improvise."

There was a long moment of silence.

"When do you want to do this?" Isabella asked.

"Yesterday."

"I'll make some phone calls and see what I can arrange." Isabella sighed. "You owe me, big time."

"Please, this is nothing for you."

"Say it."

I hesitated a moment, then exhaled, "I owe you big time. Oh, and by the way... can you give me a couple thousand in Canadian dollars? The government slaps on an extra 10% exchange fee with US dollars."

"Suck it up, buttercup. I'm not your bank."

"Okay. I see how it is."

Isabella scoffed and hung up.

I wasn't about to take the *Vivere* down to Cuba. It was probably fine, but in the event of an engine failure or other mechanical malfunction, it could end up being a long, expensive trip. Run afoul of the government, and the boat may be confiscated—neither of which I could afford.

Cobra Company had immense resources—Isabella could afford it.

She called me back a few moments later and said she'd have a boat pick me up at the marina at 6 AM. It was 90 miles to Cuba. Barring incident, I'd be there in time for breakfast.

I packed a small backpack with a change of clothes, some toiletries, baby wipes (because toilet paper is a rare find in a public restroom in Cuba), hand sanitizer, a few protein bars, and several thousand in cash. I took a small folding tactical knife with a spring assisted blade—titanium nitride coated stainless steel. It had a sleek, aggressive design, and was small enough not to raise the eyebrows of the Cuban Aduana (Customs).

Haley had listened to the call. "You're really going down there to get him?"

I nodded.

"I want to go with you."

"No, you don't. This could get ugly."

She looked at me curiously.

"If the Cuban government gets wind of the fact that I'm trying to extradite a fugitive back to the United States, I'll be arrested and thrown in jail—*if* I'm lucky. If I'm not lucky, I will cease to exist. And if you're with me... you might suffer the same."

Haley cringed.

In the morning, the *Go-Fast* boat Isabella sent burbled into the marina. It sounded like a caged lion. It was a 52' purebred racing boat with a 9'6" beam and a height of 8'. It had a deep V hull, a draft of 38", and a fuel capacity of 300 gallons. The hull was designed using computational fluid dynamics, and the boat had an extremely low center of gravity. It was rock-solid at high-speed.

This thing was fast.

It comfortably seated six passengers with bolstered leather seats. There was a lot of carbon fiber. It was the ultimate performance boat. Powered by two Mercury racing 1550/1350QC4v dual calibration engines with dry sump. There were flush mounted display screens, a carbon fiber engine hatch and air intakes, and an anodized billet aluminum swim platform. It had a top speed of 145 MPH, when in sport engine mode.

I climbed into the sleek vessel and prepared for the ride of my life.

The driver wore mirrored shades and zinc oxide on his nose. He handed me a manilla envelope that contained a passport, a travel license, and Coast Guard Form 3300 (which usually took a few weeks to get).

The driver didn't say a word, and neither did I.

He idled the boat out of the marina, then throttled up and brought the beast on plane. We skimmed across the water, barely touching the surface. The engines howled, and the wind whipped around the aerodynamic design. The acceleration pinned me against the seat.

This was pure adrenaline.

Nothing on the water could touch us.

An hour later, we pulled into the Ernesto Marina, just a few miles west of Havana. It was composed of three canals and could accommodate around 100 boats. We pulled alongside the concrete dock, and the driver finally spoke. "How long is your visit?"

I shrugged.

He gave me his cell phone number. "I'll be at the hotel under the name Steve Cannon."

The dockhands helped us tie off, and we were quickly greeted by the dock master and a doctor. They boarded the boat, searched below deck, then asked questions. The doctor took our temperature and asked if we had any diseases.

Once he was satisfied we weren't carrying Ebola, he allowed us to leave the boat. Everyone I had encountered spoke passable English. I tipped everyone $5 USD, for good measure. The dock master took our passports and escorted us to customs. I was traveling under an assumed name —*John Anderson.*

The marina wasn't the most well-maintained place in the world. There were cracks in the concrete walkway, and trash tumbled with the breeze. There was a hotel and several restaurants nearby. It was built in the '50s and was definitely showing its age. At one time, it had been the height of luxury. Now it was just a relic of a bygone era.

I bought a visa for $25 and filled out the green and yellow form. I also had to buy travelers health insurance. The cost was minimal. The place wasn't very busy, and the line was short. The customs officer greeted me with a stern face. "What is your business in Cuba?"

"I'm here to enjoy the food, drinks, and nightlife."

"Have you been to Cuba before?"

"No," I lied.

I knew they had records of visitor travel, but this was a clean passport. *John Anderson* had never been to Cuba before.

The customs agent studied the passport, then studied my face. He scrutinized my features meticulously. Once he seemed satisfied, he granted me entry. I moved to the exchange kiosk and traded dollars for CUC's. Cuba has two types of currency—one for locals (Moneda Nacional), and one for tourists. The CUC's, or convertible pesos, were roughly on a 1:1 exchange rate with the dollar. The government took a hefty 10% exchange fee—just another subtle little jab at the United States for all the animosity over the years.

Steve Cannon cleared customs shortly after I did. We made it through in under an hour. Steve told me he would check into the hotel at the marina and wait for my call. He just drove the boat—the rest was up to me.

Cabs were easy to find. They were mostly classic American cars from the '50s, painted in vibrant colors. I hopped into a sea-foam green '57 Chevy. The driver spoke English. I told him I wanted to go to Old Havana. We negotiated the fee upfront—*always a good idea.*

He smiled and mashed his foot to the floor. The engine rumbled, and the car zipped through the old world.

41

Founded by the Spanish in 1519, Old Havana served as a waypoint for the treasure bearing Spanish Galleons. I couldn't help but think of Jack, and his quest to find the lost treasure of Jacques De La Fontaine. I hoped that he would return to the hunt soon.

The city was like stepping into a time capsule. The architecture was a mix of Spanish Colonial, French, and Baroque. Many buildings were painted in vibrant hues of yellow, teal, and pink. This was the Havana meant to be seen by tourists. It was very different from the real Cuba that suffered more than half a century under an oppressive regime. This was the Havana that was broadcast to the world as a tourist destination by social media mavens and travel bloggers.

The Hotel Castillo was located at the edge of Old Havana near Parque Central. It had convenient access to the tourist sites. As one of the oldest hotels in Havana, it was full of history. The long list of famous guests was staggering. Though dated, and a bit run down, the colonial-style hotel had its charm—a street-side colonnade, high vaulted ceilings in the lobby, working elevators, air conditioning, and a complimentary breakfast that was out of this world. The three-story building had a rooftop pool and bar. Salsa music started at 9 PM and played throughout the night. The price was decent, the staff was friendly, and the food was good. Stepping into the lobby was like stepping onto the set of a movie from the 1950s.

I glanced around, scanning for my target. The lobby was filled with tourists from all over the world, though there weren't many Americans these days since the restrictions on travel had been reinstated.

The front desk didn't have a record of Gardner's stay. He had probably checked in under an assumed name. I took a seat in the lobby and watched the flow of visitors coming and going. I knew if I sat in the lobby long enough, I'd see my prey. Despite hotel records, I knew Gardner was somewhere in this hotel. Isabella had confirmed it with the cellular data from his burner phone.

Within 15 minutes, Gardner had stepped off the elevator and strolled toward the restaurant for breakfast.

My heart pounded with anticipation.

I waited for another 30 minutes as he ate.

When he emerged from the restaurant, I followed him to the elevator bank as he returned to his room.

"Could you hold the door?" I shouted, slipping into the elevator before it slid shut.

Gardner pressed floor number three, and the button lit up.

"What floor?" he asked.

"Three," I said.

We rode up in silence for a moment.

"Such a great hotel, isn't it?" I said.

Gardner flashed a courteous smile. "It is. My favorite in all of Havana."

The bell dinged, and the elevator doors slid open. We stepped into the hallway. Gardner went one way, I went the other. I walked slowly toward the end of the hall, pretending to fumble for my keys.

I heard Gardner's keys jingle, and I looked back over my shoulder to see him entering suite #305. He closed and latched the door behind him.

I plotted my next move.

I jogged down the hall and stood outside of Gardner's suite. I used an infrared attachment on my phone to get a view inside the room. An orange and red blob appeared on the screen. The darker areas appeared in tones of blue and violet. Gardner stepped into the bathroom and took a seat. The coffee had done its work.

The elevator bell rang again.

A couple stepped off the lift and strolled down the hallway, talking about their plans for the day, speaking in German.

I tried to act casual as they passed by.

They slipped into a suite at the end of the hall.

I pulled out my phone again and scanned Gardner's room. It faced the street, overlooking the park. There was a small balcony. Gardner finished his business, then stepped to the bed. He grabbed something from the desk and headed for the door.

I stuffed the phone in my pocket and flattened my back against the wall.

The door handle twisted, and Gardner pulled open the door. As he stepped into the hallway, I elbowed him in the face, shattering his nose. Blood spewed all over his white linen suit.

I pushed into the suite and slammed the door behind me. Gardner tumbled back clutching his broken face.

The good doctor apparently had some martial arts training.

He took a combat stance, then did a roundhouse kick as I advanced.

I blocked the kick, then planted my heel into his groin. He buckled to his knees with a groan. Then he yanked his leg free and scampered toward the desk. He grabbed a letter opener, sprang to his feet and twisted around, squaring off again.

He charged at me with the makeshift weapon, slashing wildly.

The edges were dull. The only thing I had to worry about was the point.

He advanced, pushing me back toward the French doors which led to the balcony.

He stabbed the tip toward my abdomen.

I twisted to the side, grabbed his arm, and pinned it against my body. I punched two hard lefts to his rib cage, then kneed him in the groin again.

He doubled over in pain.

He came up with a hard left hook that smacked the side of my face.

It wrenched my neck aside.

We twisted around as we struggled. I still clutched his arm tight against my body, neutralizing the weapon.

He continued to pummel my cheek with his fist. His knuckles smacked into my cheek.

I continued to hammer his kidneys.

We traded a few punches, then I felt a searing pain in my lower right quadrant. The tip of the letter opener had jabbed into my belly.

My jaw tightened. Adrenaline coursed through my veins, and rage swelled within. I summoned all of my strength and drove him back. I shoved Gardner onto the narrow balcony, through the French doors that were wide open.

Gardner tumbled back, hitting the hundred-year-old wrought-iron railing. His momentum carried him over.

He tumbled through the air, and a terrible scream escaped his lungs as he plummeted three stories to the street below.

I stayed inside the hotel room. There was no need to look. I heard the wet slap of his skull against the sidewalk.

There were shrieks and gasps from tourists below.

I glanced down to my stomach. It felt like I had been jabbed with a hot poker. Crimson blood blossomed on my shirt.

My hand clutched the wound, applying pressure, trying to stem the tide.

Son-of-a-bitch!

An abdominal wound was the last thing I needed.

Blood seeped through my fingers. I glanced around for something to mop it up with. There wasn't anything readily available, so I staggered to the bathroom and grabbed a washcloth. I folded it up and mashed it against my belly. Blood stained the white rag quickly.

I lifted my shirt and dug my finger into the wound, feeling around for damage. The tip of the letter opener was dull in comparison to a tactical knife. It penetrated my skin and muscle belly, piercing through my external and internal oblique. It seemed to stop at the transverse abdominis. From what I could tell it didn't puncture the peritoneal cavity.

That would've been bad.

Abdominal wounds are at high risk for infection.

I threw the blood-soaked washcloth in the trash, then grabbed another and sopped up more oozing blood from the wound.

I didn't have time for this. I needed to get the hell out of there.

I grabbed a coat from the closet. It was a little tight, but it wasn't stained with blood, and would cover the wound at a glance. I kept the washcloth between the wound and the coat and squeezed my arm against the fabric to hold it all together. Then I grabbed a white Fedora that was sitting atop a bed, put it on my head, and pulled the brim low.

I stepped out of the hotel room, strolled down the hallway, and pushed into the stairwell. I spiraled down to the first floor, casually strolled across the lobby, and exited onto the sidewalk.

A crowd gathered, circling Gardner's mutilated body that lay amid a pool of crimson blood.

I gave the body a passing glance, like every other morbidly obsessed tourist, then strolled down the street like nothing had happened.

I would have much preferred to see Gardner sit in a cell the remainder of his days. But I couldn't complain about his ultimate demise.

I flagged down a red convertible Chevy, and the taxi driver whisked me away from the scene. I didn't even get to enjoy breakfast at the Castillo.

I grimaced as I sat in the back of the cab bleeding. My skin was pale, and a cold sweat broke out on my face.

"Are you okay?" the cabdriver asked, looking in the rearview mirror with concerned eyes.

The wound needed attention. There was no denying it. The question I needed to answer was, *could it wait until I got back to the States?*

42

The Clínica Central Cira Garcia Hospital was the facility that treated all tourists with health insurance. My mind ran through all the possibilities. Showing up in a hospital with a stab wound might draw unwanted questions. And I needed to get out of the country as fast as possible before someone connected me with Gardner.

I told the cab driver to take me to the marina. I called Steve Cannon and told him we'd be making a hasty departure. 20 minutes later, the cab driver dropped me off, and I staggered down the cracked concrete dock to the *Go Fast* boat, trying not to look like a zombie. The blood flow had slowed, and the jacket did a good job of hiding the wound.

I grimaced as I climbed aboard the boat.

"You look like shit," Steve said.

"Thanks," I muttered.

He cranked up the massive engines, and the exhaust

burbled. I cast off the lines, and Steve idled the sleek boat out of the canal. As soon as we hit open water, he throttled up and brought the boat on plane. I winced every time the hull slapped against a swell.

A little over an hour later, we pulled into the marina at *Diver Down*. By that time, I looked like death warmed over.

"You should probably get to a hospital," Cannon said.

I nodded. My eyes were droopy, and it felt like my life-force had been sucked out of me.

Cannon dropped me off at the dock, and I climbed from the boat and staggered toward the *Vivere*. My side burned. My shirt and the top of my pants were stained and crusty. I pulled out my phone and arranged for an Uber.

The *Go Fast* boat burbled out of the marina behind me as I made my way to the parking lot. A few minutes later, a four-door silver Honda pulled into the lot. I hopped into the backseat and told the driver to take me to the hospital.

He did a double take when he looked at me. "What happened?"

"Fishing accident."

He didn't buy it. His foot mashed the gas, and the car peeled out of the lot. We raced across the island. "You're not going to die in my car, are you?"

A weak chuckle escaped my lips. "I don't have any plans on it."

He pulled to the curb at the ER, and I staggered out of the backseat. I wasn't sure if I bled on his seats.

Inside the ER, the receptionist looked me up and down, unimpressed. She'd seen way worse on a daily basis. She called to the nurses, "We've got a bleeder."

A nurse rushed to me and escorted me to the triage area where they took vitals and asked a slew of questions. I didn't have to wait long for a room.

A nurse started me on IV antibiotics, and a technician rolled in an ultrasound machine and scanned my abdomen.

"Tell me what's going on?" Dr. Parker asked as he strolled into the room, snapping on a pair of blue nitrile gloves.

I made up a story. "I was mugged. I should have let the guy take my money, but I decided to fight."

He seemed unimpressed. "How much did he get away with?"

"100 bucks," I said.

"Well, that sure was worth it, wasn't it?"

"Clearly," I said.

The doctor examined the wound, digging around the laceration with his gloved finger. "Looks like you got lucky. Just a few layers of muscle damage. The peritoneum is intact."

He numbed the area with lidocaine, then stitched the wound. "I'm putting in a few dissolvable sutures. Ultrasound looks good. No fluid in the abdomen, and no internal organs were damaged. I'm going to give you a course of antibiotics and something for the pain. Other than being a little sore for a few days, you'll make a full recovery. If you have increased tenderness, or swelling, come back and we'll do further diagnostics. Right now, I'm not concerned." He smiled. "I'll get your discharge papers ready."

I was relieved the damage wasn't worse. Nearly half of all abdominal stab wounds are managed conservatively without the need for surgery.

The bag of IV fluids helped perk me up a bit, and I wasn't feeling nearly as light headed.

Parker tossed the gloves, washed his hands, and left the room.

The nurse gave me a stern look. "Don't think I don't recognize you. You need to stop coming in here!"

I laughed. "I'm trying."

"Try harder." She arched an eyebrow at me. "I mean, you're cute and all, and Lord knows we need the eye candy around here, but it would be a shame if something serious happened to you."

I smiled and thanked her for the compliment.

It took an hour to get discharged. When I finally hobbled out of there, I went straight to Neuro ICU to see Jack.

43

Scarlett sat in a chair near Jack's bed. He looked the same. Terrible. The ventilator still wheezed, and an array of tubes curled out of his nose and mouth. I hovered in the doorway a moment before Scarlett noticed me. When she did, her eyes widened, and she sprang from her chair. She darted across the room to give me a hug, then halted halfway, seeing my blood-stained clothes. "Oh, my God! What happened?"

"It's nothing. I'm fine."

"Doesn't look like nothing."

"You should see the other guy."

Her eyes met mine with a curious gaze.

"I got the son-of-a-bitch."

A relieved exhale escaped her lips.

"How is Jack?"

She glanced to the bed and shrugged. "Stable, I guess.

Maybe it's my imagination, but I think he squeezed my hand when I told him I loved him."

I forced a grim smile. "Hang in there, kid. He's going to pull through."

She replied with an optimistic nod, but I could see in her eyes she wasn't so sure.

Neither was I.

"I'm a little wrecked. I'm going back home. Chill out for little while. Let me know if you need anything."

"Take care of yourself, Tyson. I can't lose both of you."

"You not losing anybody," I assured.

We said our goodbyes, and I caught a cab to the pharmacy and filled my prescriptions. I got some waterproof bandages to put over the wound so I could take a shower. Parker had told me to follow up with my regular doctor in two weeks. The main thing was to keep the wound free of infection.

By the time I got back to the Vivere, I was tired, sore, and hungry. I had gone to Cuba and back and didn't even have a mojito. I stepped aboard the boat and into the salon. Buddy greeted me excitedly. I had to keep his paws and his nails away from my wound as he pounced. "Easy there, boy."

It hurt to bend over and pet him.

I made my way gingerly downstairs, peeled off my clothes, put on the waterproof bandage, and climbed into the shower. Once again, I let the hot water wash away the chaos. Afterward, I put on a change of clothes, popped a pain pill, and made my way to *Diver Down*.

I took a seat at the bar, and Madison eyed me curiously. "Are you okay?"

I smiled. "Just tired."

"Can I get you anything?"

"Beef burrito and a mojito."

"Coming right up." She spun around and sent the order to the kitchen.

Emma Steele came on the screen behind the bar with a breaking news update. "Sources have confirmed that Dr. Gardner, wanted for Medicare fraud in a bizarre murder for hire plot was killed today in a three-story fall from a balcony at a Cuban hotel. He had been granted political asylum by the government. In other news..."

Harlan gave me a knowing glance and a wink. "Fall from a balcony, eh?"

I smiled.

My phone buzzed. I pulled it from my pocket and swiped the screen.

"I heard you ran into complications," Isabella said.

"Nothing serious."

"That's not what I hear. I need you fit. You are going to escort a client to Medellín, provide security, and ensure his safe return."

"I need a few days at least. Don't worry, I'll be tip top soon."

"I'll be in touch. Don't expect much notice. We're trying to keep the client's movements as random and as unpredictable as possible."

"Holler when you need me," I said. "Any more information on Esteban Rivera?"

"From what I can tell, he's still in Medellín."

"Good."

"How is Jack?"

I was surprised Isabella asked. "The same."

"The same is better than worse."

"Agreed. Any word on my other predicament?"

"Hang tight. I'm digging. I'll find dirt on Easton. Don't worry."

She hung up, and I spent the next few days anticipating an emergency phone call from her.

I had to be back in Los Angeles at the end of the month to face criminal charges. If she didn't come up with anything on Easton soon, this cozy little life I had built for myself here in Coconut Key would crumble.

I needed to let it all slide. There was nothing I could do about it, anyway. And the stress wasn't doing me any good. I wasn't sleeping well at night because of it. That, and the fact that my belly hurt every time I flexed.

Haley moved back to her grandfather's house and contemplated putting it on the market. When we talked on the phone, she said, "I just wanted to thank you again for everything that you and Jack have done. If there's anything I can do to help you, or him, please let me know."

"I will. Thank you. When are you going back to Miami?"

"I don't know. I'm torn. I talked to a listing agent today, but I couldn't go through with putting the house up for sale. There are so many memories here. Besides, this place kind of grows on you. I don't know. I may stay in Coconut Key for a little while." She had a cheery tone in her voice. "Anyway, I think I owe you a few beers. Let me know when you want to collect."

I smiled and said goodbye. She didn't owe me anything, but I was happy to have a few beers with her anytime.

Things were starting to settle down in Coconut Key. But I knew it wouldn't stay that way. Daniels had picked up his father from Texas and put him in a facility that we all thoroughly researched beforehand. He had a tough road ahead, but at least his father was close by and was in good care.

Scarlett called. There was a tone in her voice that I hadn't heard in a long time. "Hey, I've got someone who wants to talk to you."

Jack's voice blared through the speakerphone. "It's official. I'm invincible. Nothing can kill me!"

I breathed a sigh of relief. "It's good to hear your voice!"

"Man, I had the craziest dreams."

"Well, you were in a medically induced coma."

"The last couple weeks are like a black hole. Scarlett told me somebody took a crowbar to my head, but I don't remember a thing. I'm guessing the crowbar got bent on this thick noggin." He paused. "I just need to know one thing... Did we get who we were after?"

"I'll fill you in on all the details." I told him I would get to the hospital to visit shortly. When I hung up the phone, I let out a deep breath. A huge weight had been lifted. It was good to know I still had a best friend.

Ready for more?

Join my newsletter and find out what happens next!

AUTHOR'S NOTE

Thanks for all the great reviews!

I've got more adventures for Tyson and JD. Stay tuned.

If you liked this book, let me know with a review on Amazon.

Thanks for reading!

—*Tripp*

TYSON WILD

Wild Ocean

Wild Justice

Wild Rivera

Wild Tide

Wild Rain

Wild Captive

Wild Killer

Wild Honor

Wild…

MAX MARS

The Orion Conspiracy

Blade of Vengeance

The Zero Code

Edge of the Abyss

Siege on Star Cruise 239

Phantom Corps

The Auriga Incident

Devastator

CONNECT WITH ME

I'm just a geek who loves to write. Follow me on Facebook.

www.trippellis.com

Made in United States
North Haven, CT
24 April 2024

51730664R00162